"Even if you can sell a few motorcycles, it's only a matter of time before you get bored with this place and want to leave again," Tara blurted.

"I can see where a city woman like you might think that," Sam reasoned, "but there's still plenty for me in Beardsly. Have you considered that folks might be a bit suspicious of *your* staying power?" The deep crease between his brows softened as he indulged in a patronizing smile.

"What's that supposed to mean?" she bristled.

"I was forced to relocate when my opportunity here dried up. But you had every advantage and every reason to stay. The folks here know the difference between being left behind and being dumped. I think they'll give me another chance. You, however, might have some charred bridges to rebuild."

Sam's insight was a punch to the solar plexus. Had she been a fool all these years, unconcerned how the hometown folks would react to her refusal to visit? She might have accepted her grandmother's challenge without seeing all the relationship repairs that would be necessary, but thanks to Sam, the blindfold was off.

Books by Mae Nunn

Love Inspired

Hearts in Bloom #254
*Sealed with a Kiss #293

*Texas Tresures

MAE NUNN

grew up in Houston and graduated from the University of Texas with a degree in communications. When she fell for a transplanted Englishman who lived in Atlanta, Mae hung up her spurs to become a Southern belle. Today she and her husband make their home with their two children in Georgia. Mae has been with a major air express company for twenty-five years, currently serving as a regional customer service manager. She began writing four years ago. When asked how she felt about being part of the Steeple Hill family, Mae summed her response up with one word—"Yeeeeeha!"

SEALED WITH A KISS

MAE NUNN

Steeple
Hill®

Published by Steeple Hill Books™

STEEPLE HILL BOOKS

Steeple
Hill®

ISBN 0-373-87303-4

SEALED WITH A KISS

Copyright © 2005 by Mae Nunn

This edition published by arrangement with Steeple Hill Books.

® and TM are trademarks of Steeple Hill Books, used under license.
Trademarks indicated with ® are registered in the United States Patent
and Trademark Office, the Canadian Trade Marks Office and in other
countries.

www.SteepleHill.com

Printed in U.S.A.

But store up for yourselves treasures in heaven, where moth and rust do not destroy, and where thieves do not break in and steal. For where your treasure is, there your heart will be also.
—*Matthew 6:20–21*

This book is dedicated to my father, Ward Cooper, and to the memory of my mother, Ruth Snyder.

I love you, Daddy. You are inspirational proof that with hard work, my personal goals can be achieved and my dreams can come true.

I miss you terribly, Mama. You taught me to believe in myself and to understand the power of my words. I owe this success to you.

My parents planted seeds of faith early in my life and for that I will be forever grateful. They gave me roots to keep me grounded and wings to let me fly.

Chapter One

The rumble of a motorcycle distracted Tara Elliott from her grandmother's graveside service. Her eyes, formerly fixed on a soggy tissue, glanced up. She peeked through damp lashes to see if others were reacting to the noise.

"Miriam Elliott will be sorely missed by the townspeople of Beardsly." Pastor Ryan raised his deep voice over the disturbance. "Her generosity and commitment to the community were unparalleled."

Tara had heard little else in the two days since her return to the east Texas town of barely five thousand residents. Condolence cards by the dozens sat on the kitchen counter in the little space not occupied by deep-fried chicken, potato salad and buttermilk biscuits. Among the locals, grease and starch still abounded as edible symbols of sympathy.

"Though Miriam celebrated her eighty-eighth birthday in April," the pastor continued louder, "she was still a vital presence at Mount Zion Church, as well as a member of the Beardsly College Board of Regents."

The leather-clad rider cut the powerful engine, the sudden silence drawing even more attention from the crowd of mourners who surrounded the green canopy. Tara squinted to make out the man's face, hidden by the dark-visored helmet. Whoever the intruder was, he would get a piece of her mind once the service ended.

"As we lay our sister in Christ to rest, may we all meditate on the ways in which she touched our lives and made our community stronger." The preacher crossed his hands before him and dropped his chin in silent reflection as recorded music filled the air.

Tara smiled through her tears at the selection her grandmother had insisted be played at her interment service. A Texan through and through, Miriam was determined to pay honor, even in death, to the state she loved.

The female country singer's husky voice drifted across the quiet cemetery, singing about her desire to go to Texas if Heaven wouldn't let cowgirls in. Tara's dear friend Lacey placed a comforting arm across the back of the chair and together she and Tara tapped their toes to the familiar chorus.

The final notes of the song were lost in thunder as the bike roared to life once again, its tires crunching the ancient road. Through a cloud of red dust kicked up from dry Texas clay, Tara watched the man square his well-defined shoulders beneath the fringed jacket and offer a nearly forgotten gesture as he disappeared through the cemetery gates.

Years ago, the snappy salute followed by a thumbs-up sign ended every economics lecture by Sam Kennesaw, the college's most popular teaching assistant. Tara covered her mouth to hide what she hoped sounded like a choked sob. In truth, it was a gasp of recognition. Understanding, Lacey squeezed Tara's hand.

"Ashes to ashes, dust to dust…" The gleaming silver casket was lowered into the grave.

Grief and confrontation often go hand in hand, and this would be no exception. On the heels of burying her only relative, it appeared Tara was destined to come face-to-face once more with the man whose academic career her grandmother had ruined nine years ago.

The man Tara had once loved with all her young heart.

Sam arrived at Wade Latimer's law office the next morning earlier than required and parked at the busy grocery across the street. Hidden among the minivans, he straddled his favorite bike and considered the meeting to come.

Why was his presence required for the reading of Miriam Elliott's will? He scrubbed a hand over a three-day growth of whiskers, exhaled and folded his arms across his chest.

At precisely 9:00 a.m., a gas-guzzling sedan pulled into the parking spot in front of the offices marked Wade Latimer, Attorney at Law. The woman who emerged was one of the black-draped mourners at yesterday's service. At first glance he almost didn't recognize her. She'd filled out, quite a lot.

She swung the massive car door closed and made her way up the fieldstone walk. The familiar auburn hair was caught back into a tight French braid, which hung past the shoulders of a conservative, black suit. The gangly girl etched into his mind's eye was gone, replaced by an impeccably dressed full-figured female with graceful curves.

He appreciated the changes. A smile of satisfaction curved his lips.

She wasn't the only one who'd changed.

Ten minutes later, a door chime inside the reception area signaled Sam's arrival.

"Good morning, sir. May I help you?" The young blonde, *college intern* written all over her fresh face, glanced up from her textbook.

He drummed his fingers on the counter before her.

"The name's Kennesaw. I have an appointment with Mr. Latimer regarding the Miriam Elliott estate."

The girl's eyes lit up with interest. "I'll see if they're ready for you, Mr. Kennesaw." She stood, smoothed her hands over her cashmere sweater and disappeared down the hallway.

He removed the dark shades and caught sight of his image in the beveled glass behind the reception desk. His departure from Houston had been rushed, allowing no time for a manicure or close shave. Not that anyone in this small-minded town would expect it.

With one glance at his shaggy hair they'd cluck their tongues and judge him a failure, no better than a latter-day hippie. Now, with a like-I-care smirk at the mirror, he ran the fingers of both hands through his thick mop, ruffling the curls free from the effects of his helmet.

Around his neck on a braided cord hung expensive eyewear, in stark contrast to his old T-shirt and frayed jeans. He'd intentionally chosen a well-worn shirt with the phrase Don't Mess with Texas emblazoned across the chest.

"Mr. Kennesaw?" The intern was back. "Mr. Latimer will see you now."

Sam had more important places to be and, beyond mild curiosity, he really didn't care about the reason for today's meeting. But the shock value of this unexpected encounter would make the trip worth his time.

* * *

"What do you mean, show Mr. Kennesaw in? I thought today's meeting was only for the two of us." Tara gripped the arms of her chair and pushed herself halfway to a standing position. Her gaze darted around the room seeking any avenue of escape other than the door that stood as the only barrier between Tara and her past.

"I'm sorry to startle you like this, Miss Elliott, but your grandmother's will gives very specific instructions about Mr. Kennesaw." Sympathy filled his brown eyes. "I feared you might be upset."

Tara's heart pounded at the mention of her former teacher's name. Knowing the object of her lifelong dreams stood a few feet away threatened to send her into a panic. She relaxed with effort into the leather chair and brushed nonexistent lint from the lap of her silk suit.

"I admit I'd have preferred some advance notice, but I'm far from upset." Aware her smile was probably unconvincing, she lifted her chin.

The door creaked open behind her, and the attorney rose. She stared at the opposite wall and occupied herself with a sip of water.

"Good morning, Mr. Kennesaw." Wade Latimer extended his hand graciously. "We spoke on the phone. It's so good of you to come on such short notice."

As the two men clasped right hands in her

peripheral vision, a breath caught in her throat at the sight of a bare, muscular arm.

"Well, it was the least I could do to repay Miss Elliott for her kindness all those years ago, don't you reckon?" Sam's question dripped with icy sarcasm.

Unsure whether the mocking words were directed at her or at the memory of her grandmother, Tara glanced toward the voice for confirmation.

"Ms. Elliott, Mr. Kennesaw, I don't believe introductions are necessary," the lawyer stated the obvious.

Sam's head jerked a curt acknowledgement.

She locked eyes with a virtual stranger.

He's changed, she thought with relief. *Thank goodness.*

She would melt on the spot if the kind, gray eyes that haunted her sleep even now had stared back. Instead, she felt his cold, steely gaze wander across her face. Not to be outdone, she returned the once-over.

As a twenty-five-year-old teaching assistant, he'd been thin and studious. He'd worn the required button-down collar shirt and geeky horn-rimmed glasses that made him all the more endearing to his female students.

All these years later, he had a shape honed by physical labor. A man's body. The long legs were trim, his shoulders and torso well developed beneath the dingy T-shirt. The pale hand that had once offered a jaunty salute at the end of each class was now work-roughened, fingertips and short nails darkly stained.

More striking than any other changes were the deep tan and five o'clock shadow that gave him a bad-boy look. Even in worn-out clothes, Sam carried an air of distinction thanks to the gray flecks in his loose roguish curls.

"Have a seat, please." Latimer gestured toward a chair, took his own behind the cherry desk, then turned to face Tara.

"As you well know, the value of your grandmother's property holdings in Beardsly was once considerable. However, in recent years, she made significant donations to charitable institutions, which lessened her overall holdings. I have them itemized for you here." He handed a sheet of figures across the desk.

Tara scanned the list, unable to prevent her eyes from bulging at the scandalous amount of money her grandmother had given away. Other than the century-old house on Sycamore and its well-known collection of antiques, there couldn't be much left.

"Were you her attorney of record when she made these contributions?" Tara hadn't counted on an inheritance from the grandmother who had taken her in at three when her own mother had died of breast cancer. However, having her only relative give away a fortune to strangers was deflating.

"Yes, but Miss Elliott was quite capable of making these decisions. Her mind was sharper than mine, right up to the end. Do you have reason to question her?"

"No." Embarrassed, she glanced at her watch. "Let's move on, please. I have a conference call with my New York office in an hour."

The lawyer cleared his throat and squinted at Sam Kennesaw. She followed his gaze. Sam slouched in the burgundy leather chair, fingers laced across his abdomen, an arrogant air of detached interest on his face.

"In that case, I'll get right to the most important portion of Miss Elliott's will." Wade Latimer perched wire-rimmed glasses on the bridge of his Roman nose.

As regards the disposition of my remaining holdings: I bequeath the contents of my home to my beloved grandchild, Tara Elliott, to dispose of as she chooses. Furthermore, Tara may occupy Sycamore House for as long as she accepts all terms of my will.

Concerning my first and favorite commercial property, the Elliott Building, it is my wish to leave this ten-thousand-square-foot structure to be co-owned, co-managed, and co-maintained by Tara Elliott and Samuel Kennesaw."

Tara sputtered on a sip of water and choked behind her hand.

Sam shifted in the chair, his interest locked on the legal document.

"What was that again?" She reached for the page. The attorney pulled it to his chest, well out of reach.

"I will give you each a certified copy of the will as soon as we finish." He nodded toward two yellow legal-size envelopes on the corner of the desk. "Now, please, allow me to continue."

Effective immediately, Tara Elliott and Samuel Kennesaw must commit their full attention, resources and energy to filling the space with profitable enterprises that will serve the financial interests of Beardsly, Texas. The two must work together in a cooperative manner at all times. If either should refuse the conditions of this gift, or fail to meet their portion of the conditions, the Elliott Building and Sycamore House will become the full possession of the other.

I know many people will find this to be an odd bequest. Let them think what they will. My granddaughter will understand why I'm doing this and that's all that matters. May God richly bless Tara and Sam.

The benediction echoed against the high ceiling.

Needing a moment to compose herself, Tara stood and turned away from the men. She stepped to the inviting warmth of the window, folded her arms and stared out at the shady street.

The town hadn't changed a bit since the afternoon college sophomore Tara Elliott announced to graduate student Sam Kennesaw that she intended to marry him one day. To cap off her bold behavior she'd stood on tiptoe to plant a chaste kiss on his unresponsive lips.

After all these years, his polite rejection was still painful. Her grandmother had stoked the pain burning through Tara's teenage heart by insisting life held too much promise to settle at nineteen for the son of their housekeeper. No amount of pleading and tears could stop Miriam from ensuring Sam would no longer be a distraction.

So, Tara thought, this is the surprise you warned me about, Grandmother. Your brilliant plan to get me and Sam to come home. Nice try, but a little too much water's run under that bridge. You've made your point. You win. Sam didn't love me then and from the blank expression in his eyes, I'd say nothing's changed.

"Mr. Kennesaw," her voice was husky with emotion. She cleared her dry throat and turned to stare into the charcoal-gray eyes.

"Please, call me Sam." He smiled insolently.

"Thanks to your granny, we're business partners. No point standing on formality now."

Tara uncrossed her arms, sweeping back the black knit jacket, positioning a fist on each hip. "You can't be taking this seriously. My grandmother never intended for you to accept her gift. This was her way of forcing us together for a few moments as a lesson to me."

Sam lifted a dark eyebrow as he glanced from Tara to the sixty-something attorney, who tapped a fountain pen on Miriam Elliott's last will and testament.

"So, what do you say, Latimer? Is this a legal document or just therapy for the little lady?"

Wade Latimer stopped tapping and struggled to suppress a smile. "It most certainly is legal. Miriam discussed her wishes on this subject with me at great length. The economy of Beardsly has been suffering for years and she believed your combined expertise is just what the town needs.

"However," Latimer continued, "she intended this to be a collective gift, requiring a partnership effort. Her conditions are firm. If you're unable to honor the terms of the will, Tara, the Elliott building and your family home will become the property of Mr. Kennesaw."

She felt the flood of familiar heat and knew she was about to blush from collarbone to hairline. All her life she'd hated the terrible affliction that made her seem as if she were burning up from the inside out. A pale face and deep auburn hair already set her apart from the tanned residents of east Texas. Every time her skin flushed red, she resembled a cartoon character about to explode.

Humiliated by the embarrassing display of emotion, she felt fine perspiration break through the skin around her nose and lips. She fought the urge to swipe it away. Instead, she closed her eyes, indulging in a deep-breathing technique and a silent prayer to get past the confrontation. She dropped her arms to her sides and expelled a pent-up breath, then fixed her eyes on Sam's expressionless gaze as he spoke.

"Are you gonna honor the terms of the will or is the property mine, lock, stock and barrel? What's it gonna be, Rusty?"

"Excuse me?" She bristled at the nickname twelve-year-old Sam had used for her on the days when he accompanied his mother to clean Sycamore House. Others had picked it up and it had stuck like bubble gum on hot pavement.

"From what I've seen, it's no wonder the town's in trouble. It could use some modernization." Sam nodded, approving of his own idea. "I'll enjoy knocking down those old places."

"That's nothing to joke about and you know it," she sputtered. "The Elliott Building is a town icon and Sycamore House qualifies to be registered as an historical landmark."

"Not for much longer. I'll have them both bull-dozed by the end of the week unless you have a better plan."

She shoved the jacket sleeves to elbow length and once more folded her arms across her chest. "I believe the terms of the will require the property to be used for profitable enterprise. What could you possibly have to offer this town?"

Sam untangled his long legs and stood. He reached for the legal envelope that contained his copies and tucked it beneath a strong arm.

"Well, let's see." His eyes narrowed as though he were thinking it over. "I'm male, I've lived in this state for thirty-four years and I have a master's degree in economics. I think that qualifies me to have an idea or two on how a Texan might spend his discretionary income. Don't you reckon?"

Her heart raced. He was serious.

If she didn't do something to end this farce, what was supposed to be a brief encounter would turn into a full-blown crisis. The owners of The Heritage, one of New York's premier auction houses, were meeting in less than a week to discuss her future with the family-owned firm. Being a no-show would not bode well for the junior associate.

She turned to Wade Latimer. "Can we at least put this off for a few months? I have a job and an apartment in New York, and I'm expected back at work by the end of the week. I'm sure Mr. Kennesaw must have obligations, as well."

"As a matter of fact, I don't," Sam drawled. "I'm between projects at the moment and the timing is perfect to start a new business venture."

"In other words, you're out of work and willing to jump on my grandmother's generosity like a chicken on a june bug." Tara surprised herself with how easily she slipped back into Southern colloquialism.

He smiled. "Couldn't have said it better myself."

Her breath caught at the sight of his even white teeth. She recalled the boy whose bicuspids had been crowded and crooked. Clearly, he'd invested whatever money he'd earned in expensive orthodontia. It was worth it. His smile, even surrounded by the scruffy whiskers, was packed with appeal.

"Besides," Sam continued, "your granny's will says 'effective immediately,' and last time I checked that meant right this minute. I don't have any intention of waitin' a few months."

"He's correct, Tara."

Incredulous, she swung around to the lawyer who continued to ruin her day.

"It was Miriam's desire that you both remain in Beardsly to assume joint development of the Elliott Building. If Mr. Kennesaw is prepared to do so, I'm afraid you have no option other than full cooperation."

Wade Latimer would not be her ally. If anything, he seemed to be goading her into accepting the challenge.

"Is there another office where I can have some privacy to use the phone?" Her mind churned over the growing list of details that would have to be handled right away. She seemed to have no choice but to submit to this bizarre arrangement in order to protect her grandmother's beloved properties from destruction.

And how was Tara to interpret this twist of fate? Was it just her meddling grandmother or the hand of God on her life?

Latimer moved from behind his desk and gestured toward the door. "Of course, Miss Elliott. Come with me." He nodded at Sam. "Excuse us, please."

Sam watched the heavy door close after them with a solid thud. He pulled the envelope from beneath his arm and withdrew the document inside. A quick scan of the pages confirmed he was, for all intents and purposes, Tara Elliott's new business partner.

Tara Elliott. She'd always be Rusty to him.

He'd admired the enchanting, bashful girl most of his life, but, at his mother's insistence, always from afar. Stubborn as a child and strong-willed as a college student, Rusty had been the one to cross the line, with no concern for his precarious position.

A teaching assistant could hardly show romantic interest in a student and expect to remain on staff. But thanks to her spoiled-brat determination to have everything her way or no way at all, she'd destroyed his opportunity to finish his Ph.D. at Beardsly College. He had no proof, but he was certain the Elliott women were behind the turn of events that had suddenly eliminated his teaching position. And his livelihood.

It was a betrayal he'd never forgive.

Every day he thanked his lucky stars for his boyhood inclination to tear down and rebuild his bike when it broke down. In Houston he'd hit pay dirt with a marketable skill at motorcycle repair.

He glanced toward the papers clutched in his fist. As the shadow of an idea took shape, he grinned at his stained fingernails. Wouldn't Tara cringe when he removed the Elliott Building's back entrance to accommodate wide, overhead doors? And wouldn't her flawless complexion bloom with red blotches when he knocked out the front wall to install showroom windows?

Persuading his business manager to oversee his organization in Houston while he moved back to Beardsly to pose as Miriam Elliott's needy beneficiary was going to be a pain. But it would be worth it.

The day Tara Elliott had convinced her grandma to avenge a schoolgirl's hurt feelings was the day his life had changed. Forever.

Dealing back a bitter taste of the rich girl's medicine would be sweet revenge.

Chapter Two

The walnut armoire, one of Tara's favorites, was an elegantly carved, Louis XIV cabinet with paneled doors and original nineteenth-century hardware. As a youngster she'd always suspected her grandmother's furnishings were valuable. After earning a degree in art history and serving for several years as an appraiser's apprentice, her suspicions were confirmed. Miriam Elliott had left behind a small fortune in antiques.

Tara's hand slid across the cool, shining wood as she inhaled the pleasant, musky scent. Stacked on the shelves of the treasured piece were fragments of her childhood. Primitive artwork, English assignments, class photos and the remains of a shattered porcelain vase. Items that should have been thrown away years ago. She was grateful for the tender sentiments it revealed about her no-nonsense grandmother.

Their relationship had been turbulent since Tara's show of independence had taken her to New York City following Sam's departure from Beardsly. She deeply regretted confiding in her grandmother and couldn't bear to stay in the town where Miriam El- liott's influence had cost an innocent man his career.

At first, her grandmother had refused to support Tara's desire to live so far from home. Once she proved able to make it on her own, financial help was offered to smooth the way. But she rejected any encroachment on her freedom.

Waiting tables seven days a week forced Tara out of her introverted shell. The work paid for a tiny sub- let apartment and covered tuition for the remaining classes she needed at NYU. She embraced city life, shunning even brief visits to Beardsly. The two women talked often on the phone, but saw one another only during her grandmother's trips to New York.

Tara stood before the open armoire, acknowledg- ing that even in death, the wily old woman had left many messages before going to her grave. She had always had the last word. She'd hinted that a reunion for the young people was inevitable, but Tara hadn't dreamed that Miriam would do something so outra- geous.

After several hours of reading and rereading the papers, and finding no confusing legalese to dispute,

Tara prayed for wisdom on how to meet the challenge. The choices were limited: dive into the project or lose the last of her family ties.

She considered giving it all to Sam. Her grandmother's determination to ensure nothing developed between them had upended his conservatively mapped-out life. Maybe he deserved the remainder of Miriam's property as compensation. Then Tara recalled his cavalier threat to demolish the landmark buildings.

She closed the carved walnut cabinet. She owed everything to the generosity of her grandmother. She had risked a carefully crafted reputation to offer hope to a frightened child. Tara could never let the town of Beardsly forget the sacrifice that was bigger than the scandal.

Miriam had willingly dispelled her "old maid" image and opened her guarded past to scrutiny when she'd come to the rescue of the illegitimate daughter Miriam had given up at birth. The unwed stranger, who was dying of breast cancer, had sought out her birth mother as a final act of love. She pleaded for a home for her painfully shy toddler, determined that her child would know her true roots. The unselfish agreement between the two women had changed a carrot-topped girl's otherwise tragic future.

There was no choice at all. Tara set her sights on preserving what was left of Miriam's reputation.

The life of service to others was marred only by an action against Sam Kennesaw that she seemed determined to correct with this crazy partnership.

The French mantel clock chimed four times and resumed its soft ticking. Tara hurried through the entryway to the front door, giving a last glance at her appearance in the mirrored hall tree. As usual, wavy red wisps managed to escape the somber braid. Attempting to plaster them into submission, she licked fingertips and brushed moisture across the errant curls.

She slammed the heavy door of the huge luxury vehicle and muttered, "I thought these things were illegal." She fumbled with the ignition and the navy blue beast purred to life. It eased out of the driveway and lumbered through the streets of town.

Passing the tired old five-and-dime store next door to the boring grocery market, she grimaced at the work of community elders who clung to traditional ways, voting down proposals that might usher in expansion and change. Frustrated young people graduated from the respected college and fled for the nearest big city, depriving Beardsly of their talent and energy. What kind of business would bridge the obvious generation gap?

"Hmm," she fell into her old habit of thinking aloud. "What can I possibly bring to the town-time-forgot that will stand out and fit in at the same time?" Having felt like a misfit most of her life, Tara knew how important it would be for her idea to seem more like part of the scenery than something entirely new. Then there was that other pesky issue.

Sam Kennesaw would be her partner.

As the brown-brick two-story building came into sight, her stomach churned. Heat crept up the back of her neck.

"This is ridiculous." She dropped her right hand from the wheel and spread her fingers across her abdomen while she inhaled through her nose and exhaled through parted lips.

"I wasn't this nervous when I asked for the summer off from work to settle Grandmother's estate. If placing my future at The Heritage in jeopardy didn't send me into a panic, a twenty-minute meeting with Sam should be a piece of cake."

She steered the land yacht into the alley and slammed on the brakes to avoid a two-wheeled chrome-and-leather monster angled across the drive. She poked her head out the window.

"Only an idiot would stop there. Are you trying to get yourself killed?" she shouted over the car's engine. "Didn't you see the parking spot out front?"

Eyebrows raised, he glanced over his shoulder regarding the ostentatious sedan.

"Yeah, I noticed it, but I figured you might need it for your limo."

She squashed down the desire to smile at his wise-guy tone and familiar drawl. Instead, she switched off the ignition and pushed open the door. Since he hadn't budged from his comfortable spot, she'd be forced to go to him.

With one leg slung over the seat of the bike and muscular arms folded across his chest, there sat the man she'd idolized since they were kids. Her heart drummed a frantic beat. Beneath the five-o'clock shadow and shaggy dark hair was a glimmer of the serious boy who had done his homework at her grandmother's kitchen table.

Obviously unaffected by her arrival, Sam resumed his apparent study of the building's rear wall. It would take the patience of Job for her to readjust to this town. Life moved at a snail's pace and the uniform of the day was jeans and a T-shirt bearing an advertisement. Sam seemed to be no exception.

"I suppose I should thank you for your consideration."

"Forget it," he assured her. "Being considerate of you is pretty low on my list."

She winced as the comment hit its mark.

"Actually," he continued, "I wanted to see the condition of the alley side first."

"That's a good idea," she recovered, glancing down the length of the building. "I have the keys to the back entrance."

A fast rifle through the black clutch produced the cluster of keys.

She stepped toward the security door, then hesitated as Sam shifted his weight off the bike. He gestured for her to continue the lead.

He followed, his nose detecting a delightful scent as he watched with genuine approval. He noted how the afternoon sun glinted off her copper hair. Here and there, strands had worked free and the natural curls leapt to life.

Uninvited, the vision of a little girl's curly red hair against a kitchen's sunny window invaded his mind's eye. He heard the spray of an aerosol can and smelled lemon furniture polish as his mother dusted in the next room. She checked on him from time to time, making sure he finished his homework while she completed her cleaning duties.

Homework wasn't half as much trouble as Miriam Elliott's pesky granddaughter, but she'd grown on him as a kid and invaded his heart as a teen. He shrugged off the familiar moment and re-focused on the steel door where his flame-haired nemesis struggled to throw the heavy bolt.

"Here, let me." He reached for the keys, tapping Tara's hand in a signal to move.

She jerked her fist against her body as if he'd soiled her.

So that's how it's gonna be. You probably think I'm just a dirty mechanic. Okay, Rusty. Works for me.

He turned the bolt, pushed the door wide and

stepped through first. A few feet inside the building he paused while his pupils adjusted to the darkness. Though the place was swept clean of the former tenant, spiderwebs indicated many months without attention. Possibility permeated the cavernous, empty space.

He faced Tara, interested in her reaction to the building.

"This place always reminded me of a dungeon," she complained. "The best light exposure is upstairs. There should be more to work with on the second floor. Maybe we'll use this main floor for storage."

"And what is it you plan to store in here, if you don't mind telling me?"

"Well, inventory mostly. Since my expertise is in antiques, I naturally want to sell vintage furnishings."

"Is that so?" He crossed his arms and waited, amazed at her new air of self-confidence. "And how does that meet the requirements of a 'profitable enterprise that will serve the financial interests of Beardsly, Texas'?" He quoted from the will.

"A lot of consumers stay away from antiques either because they think they can't afford them, or they don't know anything about them."

Tara's eyes flashed a spark of excitement in the dark room. "If you know where and what to search for, Southern collectibles are quite valuable."

He couldn't resist squashing her idea like a bug. "Before you wear your arm out patting yourself on the back, you might want to consider selling something besides old furniture in an old town. Not exactly a commodity that's in short supply."

The slight droop in her shoulders said he'd driven home the supply-and-demand theory he'd taught hundreds of college freshmen.

"I hope the second floor works for whatever you sell. Just don't get any ideas about keeping your inventory down here. I have a business plan of my own."

"But I'm sure I'll need this space, too," she insisted.

"Now listen." He fixed her with a narrow stare. "You just called this place a dungeon and said yourself the real potential is upstairs." He had her there. "I'm willing to take the ground floor and approve of whatever you want to do with your half of the building, as long as you afford me the same courtesy. The old lady's will says we have to cooperate. If you don't plan to comply, right out of the gate, you might as well pack up and head back to New York."

He admired the determined curve of her jaw, tensed as she clenched her teeth at his intentional rudeness.

"You'd like that, wouldn't you?"

"Reckon I would." He smiled. "I didn't ask for

this opportunity, but I'm going to make the most of it. Nobody's ever given me anything in my life. I've worked hard for what I have. If you're not willing to do the same, I'll be happy to take your inheritance, princess."

Even in the darkened building he could see Tara's face begin to color. She closed her eyes and started that deep-breathing business again.

"So, what do you say?" He rushed her out of the moment of concentration. Her eyes flew wide in the middle of an openmouthed exhale. She resembled the flame hawkfish in his salt-water aquarium.

"For your information, I know quite a lot about hard work myself. Since I moved to New York, I haven't accepted a dime from my grandmother."

"Why start now and spoil your independence?" he challenged. "It's not too late to get out of Smallsville and back to your real life in the big apple."

"However twisted her logic may be, she had some purpose for what she's done and I intend to respect her wishes."

"Respect her money, you mean." He stroked his chin, pretending to consider something. "Speaking of money, why don't we sell both places, split the profits and be done with it."

"I don't plan to sell anything," Tara insisted. "That house is the only home I've ever known and I couldn't bear to part with it."

His slow applause echoed in the empty space. "I see you haven't lost your flair for melodrama. You almost had me feelin' sorry for you."

"I'm trying to tell you that whatever I figure out to do here I'll do it with all my heart. I'll put what money I have saved and all my time and energy into making it a success."

"Good, then we don't have a problem." He moved away from her to walk the first floor's perimeter, checking for any obvious plumbing or electrical-repair needs. He heard Tara's hesitant footsteps as she climbed the wide stairs leading to the second story.

"Hold on a minute and I'll get you some light." He returned with a halogen flashlight that illuminated a wide arch on the wooden staircase. "Do you want me to go up with you?"

Her gaze followed the steps upward to another heavy security door. She held out her hand for the cluster of keys. "No, thanks. I'm fine on my own," she insisted, swiping at a spiderweb dangling over her head.

"Oh, come on." He stomped ahead of her. She followed without argument.

As she'd predicted, the rooms on the second floor were in fair shape. With paint, elbow grease and some luck, Tara could make a go at whatever she came up with.

Watching her pace off the dimensions of the

rooms, he became conscious of the traitorous way his mind found her spicy scent tempting. She, however, seemed unaware of his presence, making notes on the small pad she pulled from her purse.

Engrossed in decorating ideas, she penciled on the walls indicating possible paint colors and several wallpaper styles. Light streamed in through the floor-to-ceiling windows on the west side of the building. Once those windows were cleaned, the old shutters replaced by modern wooden blinds, the place would be warm and inviting during the day.

At night, any lighted activity inside would beckon to citizens crossing the square. But what would attract college students? Hardly antiques. As much as she hated to agree, Sam was right.

There was a shuffling sound behind her. He'd been waiting quietly while she made her notes. She turned to find him still standing in the wide doorway, watching her.

"Thanks, but you don't have to wait on me."

"I can take a hint." His hand on the knob, he turned away.

"No, wait. I wasn't trying to run you off." She groaned inwardly at the poor choice of words.

Sam chuckled without humor and shook his head at the irony. "We both know you don't have to try at all when that's what you have in mind."

The past hung between them, as obvious as the

dust motes that floated through the shaft of light from the dirty windows. The need to tell Sam what had happened all those years ago pounded like a migraine in Tara's head. They'd never make peace until it was done and he understood this bizarre arrangement was Miriam's way of putting things right.

She crossed the empty space separating them.

"Listen, Sam, we need to talk—"

He stopped her by holding up both hands, palms outward, his face unreadable.

"I don't want to hear it. It's been too many years and there's nothing you can say now that will make a difference in my life. So don't try to soothe your guilty conscience at my expense." Sam pushed his way through the metal door and let it fall shut behind him with a loud clang.

She stared at the cold metal surface, suddenly understanding. *He blames me. He thinks being forced out of Beardsly was all my doing.*

With nine years of bitterness built up, she'd never convince him otherwise.

Tara leaned against the oak griffin dining-room table, her notes and figures spread across the polished surface. Her one faithful friend, Lacey, sat with a leg folded beneath her, raising her short torso enough to reach the bag of chips in the middle of the table.

"Sam thinks what happened was entirely my fault," Tara blurted out.

Lacey's curls tossed as her head popped up. "And you didn't tell him the truth?"

Tara shook her head hard enough to rattle her senses.

"Listen," Lacey placed her hand over Tara's, "you owe Sam the truth, and then you two can begin to put all the hard feelings behind you. Maybe even start over. Together." Her smile was full of hope.

"Even if he did believe it, he'd only transfer his anger from me to Grandmother. I won't give him the ammunition to do or say anything to soil her reputation."

"After the second chance she's given him, he'll forgive her anything, don't you think?" Lacey insisted.

Forgive anything? Tara hadn't mastered that herself.

No matter how distant, she would never forget the angry words that still resonated in her grandmother's elegant dining room.

"How could you hurt him that way? How could you do this to me, Grandmother?"

"Listen to reason, child. You have your whole life ahead of you and I won't have you waste it on the son of my housekeeper."

"That's so unfair! He's respected in his position at the college. The kids love him and I love him, too. But you've ruined everything."

"That's where you're wrong. I've simply steered you both in different directions. If, as you insist, it's God's will for you to be with Sam, you'll find one another again one day. But you'll both spend time growing up first."

"I'll never forgive you for this!" Tara had swept her arm across the oak sideboard, sending silver and porcelain crashing to the hardwood below. She'd stared through hot tears at the shattered treasure, turned and run up the stairway.

Now Tara's gaze sought the gouged floor where the hand-sculpted Asian vase had met its demise. "How can I expect Sam to forgive her when I spent the last nine years punishing her myself?"

"You have to find it in your heart, Tara. I watched Miss Miriam volunteering so much of her time, giving away so much to charity, trying to atone. And I was the one person in town who understood why she did it. Don't let regrets steal your joy, too. Promise me you'll pray about it, okay?" Lacey asked.

"I'll put that on my prayer list along with the funds for the books I have to order." Tara changed the subject.

"Is that what you decided to add to the antiques? Books?" She narrowed her eyes as she thought it over. "I like it." Her head bobbed agreeably.

"Thanks." Tara smiled, grateful for some encouragement. "I stopped at Shoppers' Mart to get some magazines this afternoon. Standing in that dark little aisle it suddenly occurred to me it was the only place in town to buy something to read."

"There's the campus bookstore," Lacey reminded.

"And as long as I want a textbook or a paperback those two places are fine. But to thumb through a special-event cookbook or a gardening guide or a biography of a musician I'd have to drive to Dallas," Tara pointed out.

"What do you think Frieda Walker will have to say about you taking business from the college?"

"Oh, I wouldn't dare compete with the textbooks and classics she sells on campus. I'll carry contemporary genres, popular magazines and international newspapers. Maybe even a computer or two for research and online chatting.

"And here's something else I'm considering." She clasped her palms together beneath her chin in nervous anticipation of her only friend's reaction. "What if I set up a coffeehouse in one corner of the store to give the students someplace new and trendy to hang out?"

"That's perfect! They'll love it."

Tara's heart lifted at the thought of something that would bring the younger crowd into her business. "We'll serve all those great flavored coffees and they can visit with their friends like the kids do in the big chain stores. I'll use the antiques as display background for the books and collectibles and *everything* will be for sale."

"I've got to hand it to you, girl, you've thought of something for everybody," Lacey enthused.

"Now I've just got to think of a way to make up the difference between my savings account and the cost of inventory."

"You ought to consider selling some of the antiques Miss Miriam left you." Lacey surveyed the room. "Your own auction house could find you a buyer, Rusty."

"First, promise you won't call me that anymore?" Tara pleaded. "That name belongs to another lifetime, agreed?"

Lacey nodded.

"And second," Tara continued, "I'm not interested in selling anything in this house."

"This stuff is the only solid collateral you have."

Tara leaned elbows on the table and rested her face in her hands. "I don't know what to do, Lacey," she mumbled through her fingers. "If my grandmother thought for a minute I'd sell her things, she'd have donated them to charity herself."

Lacey shook her blond head in disagreement and thumbed through the will. "She didn't have any problem placing restrictions on your ownership of the Elliott Building or Sycamore House. If she hadn't meant for you to sell the antiques she'd have done the same with them. It says right here 'to dispose of as she chooses,' and that means she gave you her permission and her blessing to do whatever you have to do."

"What if I borrow against some of the most rare pieces? If I fail I can always sell them. But if my idea is a success, I'll still have my grandmother's things."

Lacey munched a potato chip and wiped the barbecue residue on her jeans. "Makes sense. Okay, let's make a few calls and see who's offering the best line of credit against collateral. By the time your inventory starts to arrive you'll have the money to pay for it."

Tara felt a smile of relief curve her mouth for the first time since learning of her grandmother's death. Already organized, she reached for her folder marked Stock and thumbed through the publishing printouts. Tomorrow she'd order books, place ads in surrounding counties for antique consignment pieces and begin the marketing research on coffee houses. Remodeling and advertising came next if she intended to meet the self-imposed grand opening in four weeks.

"What's going in on the first floor?" Lacey asked.

Tara froze. She'd been so wrapped up in her own plans that she had no idea what Sam had in mind for the ground floor of the Elliott Building. She tried to recall their conversation. He had said he was going to make the most of this opportunity, but she'd never asked him how he intended to do it. He'd agreed to anything she wanted to do and now she was committed to doing the same for him.

"Tara?" Lacey nudged her. "I said, what are Sam's plans?"

"He didn't tell me." A chill ran up Tara's spine at her vulnerable position. "But Sam knows this town and we're right on the square, so it's bound to be something conservative." She hurried on, trying to sound convincing. "He may appear rough around the edges, but he comes from a respectable background. Surely he won't do anything foolish and risk this chance to make something of himself...." Her speech faltered as she caught sight of her friend's eyes rolling upward. "Would he?"

Lacey took a short break from popping chips into her mouth. "Better hang on to your fancy pants, city girl. I think you're in for a wild ride."

Chapter Three

"Motorcycles!"

"Not just any motorcycles. The best American-made bikes ever." Sam glanced up from the makeshift drafting table, savoring the moment and the site of Tara's lovely face contorted in disgust.

"It doesn't make any difference what kind they are. They're all foul-smelling and noisy. You might as well sell kerosene and chain saws down here." Tara swept an arm toward the empty first floor, soon to be occupied by Sam's Cycles. "Come on Sam, you can't be serious about this."

"I'm quite serious."

"Then you're doing it to spite me."

He rolled his eyes and snorted. "You need to get over yourself, Rusty. Not everything's about you. Did you consider consulting with me about any of your plans?"

She drew a breath to speak, but he ignored it and continued.

"No, because you want to do what interests *you*. Well, bikes are what interest me. Since it's a subject I know a little something about, I intend to make a living selling them right here in the Elliott Building. By the way," he paused, considering a new subject, "I'd like to talk to you about changing the name to the Kennesaw Building."

"How dare you." Her azure eyes bulged.

"I dare because it's time to bring this town into the new millennium. Modernize. Move with the times, don't you reckon?"

"Are you quite finished?"

"Honey, I'm just gettin' started." Sam smiled and looked her up and down. Instead of shrinking from his gaze, she stood taller and squared her shoulders beneath the solid black ensemble. He expected a battle and it seemed she wouldn't disappoint.

"Grandmother wanted us to come back here and do something to help the community. I can think of a hundred reasons why you're wasting your time trying to sell motorcycles."

"Name three," he challenged.

"Well, first of all, nobody around here rides those things."

"Yet," he countered. "And that's because they don't have a local dealer or service center. Once that objection is eliminated, you're gonna see bikers everywhere."

Tara grimaced at the suggestion. "And secondly, you'll never make any money at it. How are you going to afford all those greasy parts, let alone new stuff?"

"I have *connections*." He gave Tara a conspiratorial wink. "I happen to have a very successful contact in the business who can front me the stock as long as I can meet the, um, payment arrangements."

"And if you can't?" Her forehead wrinkled with apparent concern.

"I'd sooner not think about that." He dismissed the subject with an exaggerated shudder. "Besides, I have a hunch Sam's Cycles will be a hit."

"Well, a hunch is not sufficient reason to go into business. You need something sensible to draw customers."

"Like expensive antiques, huh? I reckon that's just what we need to get this depressed economy back on track."

She held up a hand to slow his argument. "You made that point with me yesterday and I've reconsidered my original plans. Thanks to your comments there will be a variety of products in *all* price ranges. So, I guess I owe you one."

"That's the understatement of the decade."

She ignored his jab. "I'm also going to sell a wide range of books and other reading materials, and there will be a modern coffee bar. I intend to have something for every level of spending."

"And you've done extensive market research to confirm that adding books and coffee will attract buyers by the score, I presume?" He enjoyed the flicker of annoyance in her stormy blue eyes.

"You only ask that because you think *you* know the answer. However, I have years of study and experience in appraisal and sales. I'm studying the markup on the merchandise I expect to carry, I know what the folks around here can afford to spend and I have a marketing strategy to draw shoppers from other towns."

"Well, it's nice to know my days as a teaching assistant weren't completely wasted. Sounds like you didn't spend all your time in Economics 101 daydreaming about being my bride."

He was never going to let her forget her uncharacteristically bold confession and the subsequent kiss. And, it seemed, he would use it against her.

"If you intend to humiliate me at every turn, this has no chance of being a cooperative effort."

"If you're waiting for an apology, don't waste your time or mine. I have a lot to do in the next few weeks." Sam dipped his head and resumed drawing on the large pad of graph paper, which lay atop his makeshift desk, a sheet of plywood balanced over two sawhorses.

* * *

Tara's eyes followed the movement of his thick mahogany mane as his head dropped forward. The devastating appeal of his clean-shaven profile was undermining her determination to remain calm. Against her better judgment, she admired the tanned arms stretched forward across the drawing. Her attention was drawn to the white paper where Sam was positioning windows and doors against a solid wall.

"How about number three?" she asked.

"What?" He glanced up, a puzzled expression in his eyes.

"You told me to name three reasons. Don't you want to hear number three?"

The confusion left his face, replaced by a look of expectation. Sam sat tall on the stool he'd fashioned from concrete blocks, folded his arms and cocked his handsome head to one side as he waited.

She had his full attention and no idea what to say next. "Even if you can sell a few motorcycles, it's only a matter of time before you get bored with this place and want to leave again," she blurted.

The deep crease between his brows softened as he dropped his arms to his sides and indulged in a slow shoulder roll followed by a patronizing smile.

"I can see where a city woman like you might think that," Sam reasoned, "but there's still plenty for me in Beardsly. But have you considered that folks might be a bit suspicious of *your* staying power?"

"What's that supposed to mean?" She bristled.

"I was forced to relocate when my opportunity here dried up. But you had every advantage and every reason to stay. These folks may talk slow but their minds work just fine. They know the difference between being left behind and being dumped. I think they'll give me another chance. You, however, might have some charred bridges to rebuild."

Sam's insight was a punch to the solar plexus. Had she been a fool all these years, unconcerned about how the hometown folks would react to her refusal to visit? Suddenly she envisioned her grand opening with no one to sample her fancy cappuccino, no kind face to purchase her hardbound books, no supporters to guide well-heeled shoppers her way.

She knew a thing or two about changing. She might have accepted her grandmother's challenge without seeing all the relationship repairs that would be necessary but, thanks to Sam, the blindfold was off.

She had a name for her store. Bridges to build. Literally.

Five days after her loan application was accepted, Tara was still without funds. Buying on credit and scrimping to cover her few personal needs brought back memories of her early years in the city, years she'd sooner remember with distant nostalgia than with familiar clarity.

Sam made building an exterior entrance for the second floor his top priority. By the end of today she would no longer need to bother him for passage upstairs. The thought of not seeing him at his home-made drafting table made her heart sink a bit. But it was just as well, since he goaded her at every turn.

Sitting behind the scarred secretarial desk she'd picked up at a local thrift shop, Tara's best sales voice echoed in the otherwise empty room.

"Miss Frieda." Tara tried to sound confident. "I assure you Bridges will pose no threat to the campus bookstore traffic. If anything, we'll work in concert with you to fully meet the needs of the students."

"Young lady, as you may recall, I've been 'fully' meeting the needs of my students for almost forty years, now. Did you ever lack for anything during your school days in Beardsly?"

Her fear was confirmed. The woman at the other end of the telephone line had an ax to grind.

"No, ma'am, of course not. I wanted to tell you myself about the opening of Bridges and let you know my intention is not to compete with your sales, but rather to offer literary alternatives."

"Well, you're a few days late. I've heard all about your literary alternatives."

Tara smiled to herself. So, word was out. There must be some buzz on the street.

"That nice young Sam Kennesaw already told me all about your plans."

Nice? Young? Well, by Frieda Walker's standards Tara supposed he might be.

Her smile flipped upside down. Was he secretly going behind her back to poison everybody's opinion? Was he planning to drive her out of town and keep everything for himself?

"Um, I see. So Sam gave you a call already then?" Maybe with some careful questioning she could find out what the big sneak had been up to.

"Sam? Gave me a call? Not hardly. He knows how to do things the *proper* way. He's been in the bookstore and student center every day this week. How else is everybody supposed to find out about his bike shop?"

Careful questioning of the college bookstore manager was not going to be necessary. Miss Frieda was in a chatty mood.

"And I saw him down at the Varsity Theater, too. The poor boy can't afford advertisement, but I always say word of mouth is the best mode of communication, anyway."

Tara began to suspect she was the one person in town who hadn't been the target of Sam's one-man ad campaign.

"Which is another reason for my call. I wanted

to let you know the grand opening of Bridges is scheduled for—"

"I know, June first, the same day as Sam's place, Sam's Cycles. He's already told everybody."

Everybody but Tara.

So that's what he's up to. He plans to overshadow my special day with a little excitement of his own, huh? We'll see about that.

"He's living with the students? Over in those tiny apartments?" Tara questioned.

"That's what I heard."

She and Lacey filled their plates from the all-you-can-eat salad bar at Ruthie's Kitchen. They ladled creamy dressing atop greens and choice veggies, tossing raisins and croutons on for good measure. Neither woman was inclined to pass on lunch in favor of squeezing into designer jeans. Tara's all-black, figure-minimizing wardrobe had become infamous about town. It had also become unbearably hot as the mercury rose into the nineties before noon each day.

They slid into an empty table as Lacey contin-ued. "You know the older boys don't want to live in the dorm anymore. So, three or four of them get together and share one of those little efficiencies that have less square footage than a dorm room, go figure. Well, Sam's living in the smallest one of all, which makes sense, seeing as he doesn't have a pot to cook in or a window to throw it out of."

Lacey paused to collect a getaway crouton and pop it into her waiting mouth. "Anyway, they have a new evening ritual of sitting out behind the apartments, drinking sodas and asking Sam for advice on keeping life simple. He's becoming their mentor."

At this new piece of information, Tara sucked in a surprised breath and, along with it, a raisin. Heads turned toward their table while she sputtered and coughed in an effort to dislodge the fruit. She struggled to free her airway, tears trickling over her lashes.

"Honey, are you gonna be all right?" Lacey pleaded.

Tara nodded, swiped at her running nose and continued to struggle for breath.

Strong arms grabbed her from behind, hoisted her to her feet, positioned clasped hands against her chest and gave a powerful tug in and upward. A whoosh of breath was forced from her lungs. A small projectile shot across three tables and into the trash can by the exit door.

The lunch crowd burst into cheers. She didn't need eyes to confirm what her intuition already suspected. The conquering hero was at it again.

Lacey stuffed a wad of paper napkins in Tara's hand, motioning she should wipe her face.

Sam released his grip and stepped around the table, his concern turning to amusement as Tara smeared navy mascara from one temple to the other. On the tips of her auburn lashes, he found the blue color enchanting. But by the time she'd finished wiping her eyes and nose, the streaks had given her the appearance of a masked character from the comics.

"Thank you for your help," she sniffed. "I should go to the ladies' room and freshen up."

"No, that's not necessary. You're fine, considering you were almost done in by a dried grape."

"Tara, I agree you should make that trip to the ladies' room," Lacey cautioned, gesturing toward her own eyes.

"Nonsense." Sam took Tara's hand as he sat and drew her down into her chair. "Now, finish your salad. Oh, by the way, my mama taught me to chew each bite twenty times before swallowing."

"That must be my problem. I didn't have a mama."

"No, you had a rich old grandma and I'm sure she gave you the same lecture."

He motioned for Tara to continue her meal.

"Since you mentioned your mama, how is she, Sam?"

"Fine. She married a nice retired guy a couple of years ago. They own a condo on South Padre." He crunched a crouton that he snagged from her plate.

"Aren't you having anything?" She stabbed a forkful of spinach.

"I'm waiting for the guys."

"The guys?" Tara's eyes narrowed. "Oh, you mean the students. Yes, I hear you've managed to worm your way into their living quarters."

"If you call keeping my expenses low by renting the cheapest apartment in town 'worming my way into the student quarters' then I guess you're right. Too bad Grandma didn't leave us the house together."

"But she didn't." The menacing glare was wasted in the swirls of navy that stained her eyelids and cheeks.

"That's a shame, too. Instead of rocking on your veranda at night I'm sitting on lawn chairs in the parking lot, enjoying the smell of simmering asphalt."

"Somehow, I think it suits you."

He was grateful for the excuse to smile at the ridiculous picture she made in her severe black jacket and skirt, straitlaced hairdo and birdman mask.

A mechanical roll of thunder overwhelmed the clinking of stainless on Melamine as three choppers pulled to a stop near the entrance of Ruthie's Kitchen. Burly men clad in leather removed their helmets to reveal colorful do-rags over balding heads.

Sam scooted the chair back and pushed to his feet. "Gotta go. The guys are here."

"Those men? I thought you were talking about some of the students."

"I know. You assume way too often, Rusty. And you know what they say about people who assume."

"Save your clichéd pearls of wisdom for the college boys, Sam."

"Thanks, I'll do that. I value the guidance of a woman who drinks in my every word and memorizes the lines on my face."

Tara was mortified. The man must have gone home after her humiliating teenage soliloquy and made notes. All these years she'd prayed he'd forgotten her passionate profession of love. Of the millions of forgetful men in the world, she'd had to fall for one with a razor-sharp memory.

And Sam wasn't likely to forget anytime soon. As long as she took the bait, he'd keep setting the trap.

She considered tossing her glass of ice water in his insolent face. Instead, she took a long drink to cool down the heat that threatened to rise in her throat and cheeks. She stood, picked up her black clutch and turned away.

His strong hand shot out, grasping her forearm with surprising speed. As if sensing the unnecessary pressure, Sam loosened his grip. She fixed the offending hand with a hot stare and he released his hold.

"Wait, we need to talk," he insisted. "This involves structural changes to the building that I think you should know about."

He angled his dark head toward the sound of the bikes. "Those guys are my demolition crew. Tomorrow morning their equipment will arrive and we'll begin knocking out the alley side of the building to accommodate overhead doors. The day after that we'll take out chunks of the front side and replace it with showroom windows. It'll be noisy and dusty. I didn't want to get started without showing you the drawings and explaining it all first. And I need your signature on a couple of permits."

The heat creeping up her neck couldn't be stopped by a barrel of ice water. "When did you start planning this 'demolition' as you call it?"

"About fifteen minutes after the reading of your grandma's will."

"And you're just now asking for my permission?"

Sam threw his head back and laughed. Not like you'd laugh out loud at a funny joke. More like you'd laugh with hysterical relief if you won the lottery. The lunch crowd at Ruthie's had stopped watching the commotion out front and were all staring at Sam when he caught his breath and wiped away the tears of mirth.

"You still don't get it, do ya, Rusty? I'm not asking for your permission. Not today. Not ever. I have as much right as you do to make changes to that building and if you want to drop by this afternoon, I'll give you a preview of the coming attractions. If not, I suggest you work from Sycamore House to-morrow, because it's going to be dusty when those bricks fall."

He retrieved his helmet and headed toward the exit, but he didn't exactly make a beeline for the door. Instead he worked the crowd as if he were running for office. He smiled and complimented the ladies and glad-handed all the men. If there'd been a baby in the place, he would have kissed it.

Along with everyone else, Tara found herself mesmerized by the vision of Sam and the other men beyond the plate-glass windows. Then, she caught sight of her reflection in the shiny pane. As Tara's hands flew to her face, Lacey's blond reflection joined that of the wretched blue-faced creature in the glass.

"You have to admit, I did try to get you to go to the ladies' room."

Tara opened her black clutch and withdrew a small canister of pepper spray. She handed it to her friend.

"In the future, if I ever refuse to follow your instructions, use this."

Chapter Four

By noon the next day, a hole big enough to accommodate a fire engine gaped in the back wall of the Elliott Building. Each time a sledgehammer met with the antique structure, Tara shuddered from the impact, but she was intent on watching the entire operation.

The hems of her black silk-knit slacks were coated in dust. Fine particles of baked clay clung to the tail of the matching knee-length tunic, a sign of her dogged determination to retrieve as many undamaged bricks as possible. Surely, she reasoned, some quaint and nostalgic collectible could be fashioned and sold at Bridges from the hundreds of otherwise useless blocks.

"Why don't you leave that to the crew? They'll be just as careful and you won't be picking bugs out or your hair for the rest of the day."

Sam removed a leather work glove and touched the top of her head. Waving his fingers in front of her face, he dangled a shriveled granddaddy longlegs.

She yanked off her own gloves, tossed them on the pile of rubble and brushed frantically at her crown, further dislodging hair from the already beleaguered braid.

"Oh, I hate spiders!"

"Don't get excited." It was obvious from the chuckle in his voice he was enjoying her discomfort. "The thing's been dead for ages."

"It doesn't matter. The very idea of a spider touching me makes my flesh crawl."

"I know."

"That's right, you sure do." She looked up into his dark sunglasses and, instead of obsessing over her dirty reflection, she noted the mischievous grin on his face. As a child she'd seen that smile many times, often accompanied by a silly prank.

"I figured you'd toughen up and get over that."

"I thought I might, too. Then I moved to Manhattan into an apartment that had to be the spider capital of the world. And I don't mean a few here and there that you manage with a can of bug spray. I mean millions of the creepy things spinning webs faster than I could knock them down with a broom." She shuddered from the memory.

"You wouldn't exaggerate, would you?"

"No." She swatted at the top of her head again, certain the drop of sweat that slipped down her once-careful part was an errant arachnid. "Working with antiques, you run into all kinds of insects nesting in forgotten corners. I can live with moths and carpenter ants and I don't mind the odd beetle now and again. But spiders…"

"I remember when you first came to live with your grandma." Sam removed his glasses, his eyes narrowing in concentration. "I was eight and my mama told me to be nice to you because you were Miss Elliott's granddaughter. It took me six years to work up the courage to ask how Miss Elliott came by a grandchild when she'd never been married herself."

Tara nodded, understanding the circumstances surrounding the sudden appearance of a three-year-old in spinster Miriam Elliott's life. As small as she was, even Tara could sense the heads and tongues wagging behind their backs. By the time she'd started school the scandal was old news and most of the whispering had stopped.

"Anyway, you wouldn't give me any peace till I came up with a deterrent."

"How did you know I was afraid of spiders?"

"What little girl isn't?" He smiled at the recollection of his plan. "It was worth a few minutes under the front porch to find out."

Tara grimaced at the long-buried memory. "You

were bad to bring that jar of spiders into the kitchen."

Sam tilted his head back and laughed. Again, she was struck by the appeal of his smile, her mind sweeping back to the one tender kiss she'd given him years ago.

"Hey, Sam, you want to measure this cased opening one last time to make sure we've got it wide enough to suit you? Then we're gonna knock off for lunch."

Sam turned his back, striding away without so much as a nod. She shook off the dismissal and returned to the salvage operation. Reaching for another brick, she noted the hopelessly chipped state of once well-maintained nails.

"Oh, well," she mused aloud, "the first time I strip a cabinet with five layers of paint you'll be history anyway. Might as well throw out all my polish and trim you short."

"You still talk to yourself, I see."

Tara looked up from her conversation with her fingernails, embarrassed yet again to have Sam catch her looking foolish. She huffed out a breath of exasperation in resigned response.

Sam let her off the hook, but not for long. "Want something for lunch? Preferably without raisins. I won't be able to keep an eye on you while you eat today."

"No, thank you." She brushed the back of her

filthy hand over her brow, damp with perspiration, feeling the gritty film layered on her skin. "I'll eat something at the house. I need to change for an appointment."

"As long as you're changing anyway, why don't you wear something that's not so...not so..." He seemed to search for the right word. "Black."

She glanced down at the chic and now very dirty ensemble she'd been fortunate to acquire at a fashionable second-hand shop in Manhattan. She fervently hoped the fabric's thick covering of red dust was temporary.

"I'm afraid that's not possible."

"And why not?" Sam crossed his arms, waiting for a reply. She studied the muscles flexed across his chest and lost her train of thought.

"Hmm?" she mumbled.

"Why isn't it possible for you to wear something that's not black?"

"Oh, that's simple." Her eyes snapped back to his face. "Because everything I own is black."

"I kinda figured that, but so has everybody else in town."

Startled by Sam's blunt observation, she grudgingly admitted he was probably right. Her black city clothes seemed out of place in Beardsly and her skin was crying out for something light while the air-conditioning unit was being replaced. Still, she wouldn't give him the satisfaction of knowing it.

"My wardrobe is none of your concern."

"Suit yourself." Sam executed a smooth about-face to head in the direction of his friends. He shot back over his shoulder, "If you wanna spend the summer looking like an undertaker, what do I care?"

Undertaker? She snorted at the insinuation. Just because a person wore black, it hardly labeled her as a mortuary manager. Black was elegant. Black was slimming. Black was…too hot!

Fresh from the shower, Tara stood in the open door of her darkened closet. Her fingers slipped along the wall in search of the switch plate. A flip of the plastic lever coated the room with glaring light from an overhead globe. She squinted in the brightness.

As her eyes adjusted, she faced the full-length mirror on the opposite wall and grimaced at the sight of her body in baggy shorts and a tank top. Years of eating on the run and lack of exercise had added pounds to her tall frame. Under the harsh light, her bare arms appeared fleshy and pale, full thighs were in need of sun and physical activity. The all-black wardrobe concealed her flaws well.

"Exactly why I never wear anything else," she admitted.

For the millionth time, she pondered the mystery father who must have been a man of some stature. Her mother and grandmother had both been slender, so the constant struggle with twenty extra pounds in her adult years must have come from the paternal gene pool. It wasn't fair. Girls should take after their perpetual-motion mothers, not their couch-potato fathers. Making a mental note to look into a gym membership, she clicked off the light.

When the phone jangled in the hallway, she abandoned the effort to wangle her thick wad of hair into a twist. A female voice cancelled the loan officer's appointment, but confirmed the funds would be available within twenty-four hours.

Going back to the steamy confines of Bridges was out of the question. The free afternoon was a sign she should do something productive. Something useful. Something she was good at.

Shopping.

First stop, Lacey's Closet, the one ladies' boutique in town. Right out of college, Lacey had opened the store, to the excitement of the young women of Beardsly. Of course, there was always Shoppers' Mart, but Tara had sworn never again to buy clothes at the same store where a customer could also purchase a side of beef or a truckload of mulch.

Next stop would be the big flea market over in Longview. It was open until dark the first week of each month. She smiled at the thought of haggling over musty pine chests and scarred sideboards. Hopefully there wouldn't be any spiders lurking in the drawers.

* * *

"Wear your hair down."

The thought hadn't occurred to Tara in so long, she was surprised by the casual suggestion.

"When we were kids I always loved your hair. Why you insist on bunching it up like that is a mystery to me."

Without waiting for permission, Lacey removed the large pins that secured the heavy twist, and auburn curls fell in a soft cascade around bare shoulders.

The likeness in the three-way mirror was becoming. Capri pants weren't a new fashion statement, but they were a novelty to Tara's ultra-conservative wardrobe. The stretch denim fabric hugged in all the right places while leaving a flash of pale shin exposed.

"That yellow blouse is yummy with your hair color. It's so feminine."

"You sure? I thought redheads shouldn't wear yellow." Tara admired the contrast of her hair against the buttery linen, sure the scoop neckline was too daring.

"Of course they can." Lacey reached for a pair of hand-decorated sneakers. "Here, try these. You can't put those black flats back on or you'll look like a dweeb."

Tara slipped into the trendy shoes, enjoying the colorful appeal. It was a good thing she was headed outside the city limits, otherwise she'd be too self-conscious to test the new look.

With a bright blue T-shirt and a pair of crisp khaki shorts in her shopping bag, she climbed back into the mammoth sedan and headed for Rent-a-Heap-Cheap, the one truck rental in town.

"It runs great as long as you keep pouring in the oil, Miz Elliott. There's a case behind the seat. Be sure you add a can or two when you stop for gas." The rental agent smiled, slammed the door of the eighties-model pickup and waved Tara out of the gravel parking lot.

Rearview mirror adjusted, seat belt tightened, she headed south on the Longview Highway. A half hour into the drive, the truck began to sputter. A red light flashed in the cracked dash.

She steered to the shoulder of the road, catching a glimpse of her watch. Three thirty. No need to get excited. Some kind farmer would stop to render aid if she couldn't get the truck started.

First things first, she hoisted the creaky hood, a universal sign of motorist distress. After a struggle to pull the seat forward, she located the promised case of motor oil. A can opener hung from a string tied to the gun rack. She punched V-shaped holes in the tops of two cans and carried them to the front of the truck.

Now what? Stretching up on tiptoe, she leaned over the workings of the engine and tried to figure out where to pour the dark goo.

* * *

As the Deuce glided around the bend, Sam wondered what malfunction had stalled the old truck, fifty yards up ahead. When he spied the woman, poised on the balls of her feet exploring beneath the hood, the truck was soon forgotten.

He slowed and appreciated the sight the woman made; her shirt was the color of a caution sign, but it was the luxurious rust-colored hair spilling over her shoulders that caused the involuntary clenching of his fingers on the wheel. He came to a screeching halt at her heels.

He watched the shoulders sag and the head give a shake of resignation as the woman realized the identity of her Good Samaritan.

"Well, well, well. What have we here?" he taunted, removing his helmet. "Need help again, little lady?"

Holding both cans of oil, Tara straightened. Careful not to whack her head on the hood, she twisted to face him. The color in her face was already high from leaning over the warm engine. The pink tones deepened.

"Very gallant." Her eyes narrowed. "Would you please help me get this truck started so we can both be on our way?"

"Aren't you even going to ask me what I'm doing here?"

"Okay," she sighed. "What are you doing here?"

"I've been in Longview getting the word out about Sam's Cycles' grand opening. I even mentioned your place a time or two."

"I would appreciate it if you'd let me handle my own affairs."

"Hey," he held his palms out. "If you don't want the free publicity, no problemo."

"I'm sorry," Tara apologized. "I'm renting this clunker by the hour and I need to get to Longview myself to catch the last day of the flea market."

He leaned the bike against the kickstand and slid off.

"What makes you think it needs oil?" he asked. He rounded the truck bed and pulled open the driver's door.

"That red light on the dash was a dead giveaway."

He leaned out the window to get a good look at Tara.

"Did you also notice the red light that said you were out of gas?"

She closed enticing blue eyes and shook her head, a small but definite admission of guilt.

"No. The guy I rented it from mentioned adding oil when I stopped for gas. I didn't realize I was supposed to stop so soon since rentals usually come with a *full* tank."

"Well, the good news is, this is easy enough to fix." He relieved her of the oil cans, then moved to the bike and snapped a spare helmet off the back. He held the protective headgear out to Tara, enjoying the incredulous look on her face as she realized his intentions.

"Oh, no." She backed up, trapping herself between the truck's grill and his approach.

"Oh, yes. I'm not leaving you alone beside the road."

Then he gave in to something he'd longed to do since the day a grown-up Tara Elliott had stepped foot into his classroom. Sam tucked thick strands of hair behind her delicate ears, slowing long enough to enjoy the sensation of silk against his skin. Fingers lingering longer than necessary, he stared into azure depths that darkened at his touch.

Unsettled by his emotions, he recovered from the tender moment by squashing the helmet over Tara's head, careful of her exposed ears. Her mouth popped open preparing to object, so he secured and tightened the chin strap.

"You are wasting your time, Sam. I have no intention of getting on that thing." She pointed a shaking finger at the powerful machine.

"Scared?" he taunted.

"I've never been scared of anything in my life."

"How about spiders?"

"Okay, there's that," she conceded, "but otherwise I'm fearless."

"Then there's no problem. Let's go." He stepped

to the truck to collect her pocketbook and keys, and locked the dented door, not that anyone would think to vandalize the battered old work truck.

Approaching his reluctant passenger, he admired her in the colorful outfit. "Rusty," he said, smiling broadly at the picture before him. "You are some firecracker."

Tara's lips curved in a shy smile but the look in her eyes said she didn't quite believe the compliment.

He grabbed her hand, pulling her toward the bike where he stowed her belongings in a leather pouch. She stood to one side as he secured his helmet, settled himself on the seat and brought the engine to life.

"Put your left foot on that peg and throw your right leg over the seat behind me."

Worried eyes passed across Sam and the bike.

"What are you looking for?"

"Where do I hold on?"

Laughter rumbled deep in his chest. "Put your hand on my shoulder while you climb on and then wrap your arms around my waist." He might as well have a little fun. "And you'll need to hold on tight to keep from being thrown off the back when we hit bumps."

Mortified, she backed away from the bike. The look of trepidation on her face was priceless.

"I'm joking. Get on and feel free to hold on, but

not out of fear." He revved the engine and she responded by hopping into place and throwing her arms around his middle.

He rolled the throttle and her arms tightened as the bike roared onto the quiet country highway.

Anticipation curved Sam's lips into a sly smile. The woman was a tempting target and the afternoon presented some unexpected possibilities for payback.

Chapter Five

Tara clung to Sam as if her life depended on it. Chin tucked, jaw clenched and eyes squeezed shut, she held her breath and braced for the inevitable moment when she'd be hurled into space, her life snuffed out against a tall Texas pine.

She felt a rumble of sound where her chest was pressed against Sam and realized he'd spoken. She didn't dare raise her head to respond, but held on tighter.

Again the rumble, this time followed by the warmth of a comforting hand placed over the death grip she had around his taut stomach. He patted her clenched knuckles, then gave them a little shake.

Even maintaining her stiff posture she couldn't ignore the light massage he was administering to her rigid wrists and forearms. The message was obvious. Loosen up.

Chest aching from holding her breath, she exhaled through dry lips and then inhaled slowly to fill deflated lungs. Along with the oxygen came the scent, the very essence of Sam. An appealing mixture of morning soap and afternoon heat stole into her nostrils and tickled her senses.

"Well, do you like it?"

Her eyes flew open, revealing a blur of scenery streaking past them at what seemed like a hundred miles an hour.

"Do I like what?" she returned his shout.

"The ride. Isn't it great?" Sam angled his head to keep his eyes on the road while his words flew over his shoulder.

"I feel like I'm riding a guided missile."

"We're only going the speed limit. You want me to show you what she'll really do?"

"No!"

His roar of laughter coaxed a trembling smile to Tara's lips.

Sam pointed to a sign indicating an *S*-curve in the road up ahead.

"When we go into the curves, lean with the bike. Got that?"

As she nodded understanding, a right-hand bend in the road closed around them and he accelerated, angling the handlebars and his shoulder toward the pavement. Heart pounding with pure terror, she followed his lead. She gripped Sam's middle, molded her body to his and leaned with him into the curve. Before the squeal in her throat could escape, the bike entered the bottom of the *S*-bend and the two humans moved as one with the machine.

The few seconds it took to navigate the double curve seemed an eternity. The moment they were once again perpendicular with the road she opened her mouth to release a scream.

But Sam beat her to it.

"Yee-ha!" he shouted, and punched the air with his fist.

Tara understood his exhilaration.

"You okay?"

She could hear the smile in his voice. It was an endearing sound.

"I'm okay," she confirmed.

"Then let's make time."

She turned out to be a good sport, a revelation that dampened Sam's devious intentions. In fact, he was pleasantly surprised by the woman who'd once been so reluctant to try anything new.

Although he had important calls to return to associates in Houston, he made the spontaneous decision to take Tara straight to the flea market instead of stopping at the first gas station they saw. If she preferred to do otherwise she was keeping her opinion to herself.

He took the parkway around the business district

and made it to the fairgrounds well before the early birds began to pack for the drive home. The gate attendant waved them through, pure longing on his young face for the classic bike. Sam idled the bike into a shady spot and cut the engine.

"How'd you manage this?" Tara gestured toward the VIP parking sign.

He tugged at his helmet and slid off the seat. "You'd be surprised at the special treatment these motorcycles get. And that's why they're going to sell."

Tara handed over her headgear, apparently oblivious to her light case of helmet hair.

"But aren't these things expensive?" She grasped his outstretched hand and he hauled her to a standing position.

"They're not cheap, but there are bargains to be had and I intend to offer great terms."

"You're not going to use your *connections* are you, Sam? Grandmother would never have given you this opportunity if she'd thought for a moment you were involved with someone dishonorable."

Taking a step closer to Tara, he stared down into her eyes.

"Someone dishonorable," he repeated flatly. "You mean the kind of person who would use their good fortune to take advantage of others? You mean someone who might lie to serve their own purposes?" He watched her blink hard at the description. "Well, that's the connection I have right now, don't you reckon, Rusty?"

He didn't back away and she wouldn't look away. Color swept over her throat, highlighted by the bright-yellow blouse. As crimson streaks snaked across her skin, she made no effort to do her silly breathing exercises. When the warmth reached her face, she took a small step closer, pressing the tip of her index finger into his chest.

"Listen, Sam, I tried to explain and you wouldn't give me the chance."

"And I'm not going to let you *explain* it today, either." He brushed her finger away. "You can live with the consequences of what happened, just like I have."

"You think I haven't?" She bristled. The heat infused her cheeks. "I've lived with it every day for nine years."

Arms folded across his chest, he leaned back to study her. "Good. That's what I wanted to hear." He glanced down at his drug-store wristwatch. "You've got a while before they close, so get going. I'll meet you back here in two hours."

The upward jerk of her chin and the sudden glistening in her eyes told Sam nothing was settled. But it never could be as far as he was concerned.

Tara splashed cool water on her face and dabbed it with a coarse paper towel. She ran shaking fin-

gers through flattened hair, disgusted with her piti-
ful attempt to be feminine.

How on earth were they supposed to be partners
when they couldn't even be civil? Did they stand a
chance of helping the economy of a small town
when they hardly stood the chance of being friends?
What in the world was her grandmother thinking
when she came up with this scheme?

Tara pushed the troubling thoughts aside. At the
moment there was a more pressing issue to address.
She needed to secure a few eye-catching pieces to
act as the central focus for her grand opening, only
weeks away. She considered temporarily moving
some of her own antiques from the house to the
shop, but she wanted everything on display at
Bridges to be for sale.

No matter what the price, parting with the exqui-
site furnishings in Sycamore House was not an option. Yet.

Several times already, she'd made that clear to
the persistent Houston dealer who had called almost
daily since Miriam Elliott's obituary had been
picked up by the *Chronicle*. The incredible ensemble of furniture, showcased in both *Texas Living*
and *Southern Comfort* magazines was the envy of
collectors across the state. At a well-advertised sale,
it could fetch a prince's ransom. She hoped she'd
never have to resort to that plan.

She shook her head, dismissing the very idea

and began to weave her way up and down the long marketplace aisles. Dealers from surrounding states brought everything from silver to stained glass, cheap pine nightstands to Chippendale chairs.

The third-generation owners of The Heritage had hired her for her broad knowledge of collectibles, and her countless hours of study would pay off at these regional markets.

Every month shoppers saw a new round of wares. The untrained eye could be deceived. That deception ran both ways. A smooth-talking dealer could pawn off a good copy of a Tiffany lamp on an unsuspecting buyer. On the other hand, a six-hundred-dollar Roseville bowl might nestle amid garage-kiln pottery on a table labeled Nothing Over a Buck!

Thirty minutes into the search, a jiggling display of bobble-head dolls stopped her cold. Celebrity cartoon faces smiled and nodded agreeably on their springy necks. But it was the padded surface they perched upon that caught her attention.

She squatted to eye level with the tabletop and used a thumbnail to gently scratch at the surface and chip away black paint from a carved leg. It was in desperate need of stripping and refinishing, but beneath the dust, cigarette scars and coats of household lacquer was a Victorian kneehole writing desk with a tooled leather top. Restored, it would easily bring three thousand at auction.

Sitting in dilapidated lawn chairs were two seventy-something gentlemen in seersucker coveralls, mirror images of one another. She extended a hand.

"Hello, I'm Tara Elliott."

One clasped her palm in a friendly shake. "Evening ma'am. Name's Ward Carlton. This here's Walter. We're the Carlton brothers."

"Pleased to meet you, gentlemen. What are you asking for the desk?"

"Well, we don't have a price on the desk. We only sell the dolls. Right, Walter?"

Walter nodded.

"But you would consider it, wouldn't you?" She smiled at Walter.

"Don't know why not. Ward?"

"Works for me." Ward scratched his gray head and took several turns around the table. "How about thirty-five?"

"Hundred?" Tara gulped. Maybe this wasn't her day after all.

The brothers stretched their lips back over their teeth, grinned and nodded, looking like bobbleheads sprung to life.

"Point well taken, ma'am." Ward continued to chuckle. "Okay, I guess that was a bit much for this old thing. It'd been sittin' in the barn forever. I dragged it out and put a new coat of paint on it a couple years back and it makes a pretty good display table, don't you think? But it's awful heavy to get on and off the truck, even for both of us."

He pointed over his shoulder to the late-model diesel pickup.

"I think TV trays would do just as good, don't you Walter?

Walter nodded some more.

"So we'll take twenty-eight dollars, twenty-five if you have cash."

"Twenty-five *dollars*? That's all you're asking?"

Ward squinted one eye, leaned his whiskered chin against a weathered hand and rocked back on his heels to study the desk.

"You think it's worth more, ma'am?"

"After a good deal of restoration I'm certain it will command a handsome price."

"Well, that settles it. Two cans of spray paint is all the restoration it's gonna see from me or Walter. The price is twenty-five cash. Take it or leave it."

"Sold," she agreed, and handed the man two bills. "What time will you be leaving today? My rental truck ran out of gas halfway from Beardsly and I have to pick it up and come back."

"We've got a place right outside of Beardsly. We'll deliver for another five."

"Make it ten," she bartered. "Deliver the bookcases I already bought and you've got a deal."

"Make it fifteen and we'll deliver everything else you buy today, too." He rubbed leathery palms together, eyes twinkling as he anticipated the payoff.

She checked the time. "In that case, I'd better get busy."

Sam caught sight of Tara about fifty yards from the gate. Her lustrous hair, set off by the yellow blouse, made it hard to miss her. He saw others take note of her, as well. Her empty hands were evidence she'd struck out, but she strolled with a carefree spring in her step through the dwindling crowd.

The determination to maintain his foul mood fled on the breeze as wisps of her hair danced out of control. By the time she reached the bike he was mesmerized by the motion. She'd grown into a spectacular, self-confident woman. As his heart thundered at the thought, he reminded himself that his real life was on hold for some payback. Nothing more.

"No go, huh?" he asked, casually.

"On the contrary." She flashed an enchanting smile. This close he could see the way her front teeth overlapped a tiny bit. Running his tongue across a smooth bite, he remembered how embarrassingly crooked his own teeth had once been. He'd financed braces before he'd even financed his first bike.

Tara continued, "I bought several nice pieces of furniture and quite a few interesting knickknacks for Bridges."

He looked past her for some proof of the statement.

"Don't worry, everything's being delivered tomorrow. If you can take me to get some gas and drop me off at the truck I won't be any more bother. *Today,* anyway."

"What's that supposed to mean?"

"I'm going to need a little help getting the pieces up the stairs."

"Let me guess. You want *me* to do it."

"No, of course not. I thought maybe you'd allow your construction friends to help me for an hour or so. I'll pay the going rate till I can find some local boys to help out in the future."

"And what's wrong with the guys making the delivery?"

"They're a little old to be hauling heavy pieces up twenty steps. I'm sure they'd help if I asked, but to be honest, I already feel like I've taken advantage of them."

"How's that?"

"They sold me an old desk, and I'm positive there's a very nice piece beneath about ten layers of black paint."

"Did they set the price?"

"Yes. I even gave them the opportunity to raise it."

"Then you're not taking advantage." He handed her a helmet.

"I know, but they seem like such nice men, I hate making a huge profit on them."

"Get used to it. The goal of enterprise is to buy low and sell high. You're in this for the money, so save your guilt for something besides profit margins."

"You're right, and if their big truck is any indicator, the Carlton brothers do very well for themselves."

"Ward and Walter Carlton?" he asked, not believing the dumb luck.

"You know them?"

"Everybody who's lived in this state for the past three years knows them. They own Flapjack Heaven."

The auburn tips of her eyebrows tilted together.

"You mean that truck stop on the edge of town with the giant stack of pancakes for a roof? That place belongs to them?

"That one and forty-seven others across Texas."

As the news sunk in, he watched her crystal-blue eyes widen.

"That's right," he confirmed. "They could probably buy everything in both our showrooms out of pocket cash and still have money left over to put a freshman through college."

"Then what in the world are they doing selling bobble-head dolls at a flea market?"

"The Carltons aren't exactly known for their conventional business practices."

She shook her head, looking as if she felt a bit foolish.

"I guess I don't need to worry about making a killing off that desk after all."

He climbed on the bike, reached for Tara's hand, and hauled her up behind him.

"All you need to worry about right now is how you're going to pay me back tomorrow after I help haul your junk up that flight of stairs."

Before he let her soft hand slip away, he couldn't help noticing how well it fit into his much larger palm. Neither could he ignore the arms that encircled his waist.

Determined to put a barrier between his thoughts and his passenger, he brought the powerful engine to life with the push of a button. The bike's obedient response brought a smile to his face and then the mechanics of safely negotiating back roads en route to the highway occupied his mind.

But not entirely.

Chapter Six

At cruising speed and with fifteen minutes of silence stretching ahead, unwanted memories betrayed Sam.

The years hadn't dimmed the bittersweet recollection of his student's confession of love. She'd stubbornly insisted God had a plan for the two of them and she'd wait it out. To make matters worse, she'd boldly sealed the revelation with a whisper of a kiss. His heart still ached over the pain in her eyes when he'd told Tara that, under the circumstances, there could never be anything between them.

She hadn't left well enough alone that day any more than she had as a pesky child. Only this time her determination to have her way had cost him everything.

He squeezed his eyes shut for a split second to extinguish the thought.

With an explosion like a Black-Cat firecracker, the tractor-trailer up ahead blew out one of its eighteen wheels. His eyes opened wide as huge shards of rubber spewed across the road, an instant obstacle course.

"Hold tight," he shouted.

Before she could question the instruction, he accelerated, deftly navigating the debris field, confident as any downhill-slalom Olympian. He bypassed chunks of rubber, marveling as always over the aerodynamic technology of the machine he'd grown to love.

Tara's high-pitched shriek drew Sam back to reality. Certain she was terrified, he eased off the throttle, slowing to cruising speed.

"No!" she shouted.

"I'm sorry." He imagined her face bloodred with terror. "You want me to pull over?"

"No," she repeated. "Do it some more."

A warmth he'd never experienced before spread from the core of his body to the tips of his limbs. He punched the air with his fist, offered up his salute and kicked it up a notch.

In no time at all, the bike eased alongside the battered rental truck. With the music of the engine still ringing in his ears, he gripped Tara's hand to help her stand.

"That was…incredible." She tilted her face up to him, an easy smile reaching her unforgettable eyes.

"Sorry about the road gators, but they're a hazard of the sport."

"If all the hazards are that exciting, I see why you love this thing." She thrust her helmet in the direction of the bike.

He took the gear, dropped it on the seat beside his and turned to find Tara moving toward the truck, her hand slipping through the blaze of auburn hair. The urge to let his fingers do the same was uncontrollable. With a single step and a full arm's reach, his hand followed hers as it trailed through the softness. The feathery-fine silk slipped through his fingertips.

Tara lifted her face at his touch, tilting her head back so he could see into the blue depths.

His hands moved unconsciously to hold either side of her questioning face. The heat from her skin seeped into his flesh, a match for the unfamiliar warmth in his heart. He closed the inches between them and paused to moisten his dry lips before he covered her mouth with his.

The blast of a car horn shattered the magical connection.

"Hey, Sam!" The cheerful passerby waved as they stepped apart.

Tara witnessed Sam transform from helplessly involved to blatantly arrogant. He offered up his signature salute as he swaggered away and busied himself with the bike.

"Sorry about that, Rusty. You have a way of doing that to me. Something you might want to remember."

"Thanks for the warning." Her mouth tingled from the impetuous kiss.

He handed over her purse, motioning for the truck's keys. She dropped them in his open palm.

The truck shook as he pumped the gas several times and cranked the tired vehicle to life.

"I had one of the boys come fill the tank."

"That was very kind of you, Sam."

"I wasn't trying to be kind, just efficient." He held the truck door open. After she climbed up into the cab he slammed and locked the door. "Now we can both be on our way so the evening won't be a complete waste."

Tara bit the inside of her lip, determined to control the quiver that threatened. "See you tomorrow?" she asked, as he walked away.

"Don't see how it can be avoided." He tossed the comment over his shoulder, straddled the bike and angled his head for her to take the road.

As the highway widened, the bike blew past the old truck. Its rider leaned forward, alert to the road, muscles taut, obviously intent on putting distance between the two vehicles.

Clearly she wasn't the only one suffering the effects of the brief kiss. For almost a decade her dream was dormant. But it dared to sprout a tiny bud as she offered up a prayer of hope from inside the old truck.

Six days and as many delivery trucks later, Bridges was bulging with cartons and furnishings. By night, Tara painted, papered and hand-stenciled the walls of her shop. By day she arranged collectible volumes on hundred-year-old bookcases, piled inviting hardbacks on the shelves of family-heirloom pie safes and arranged pine tables and cushioned chairs in groupings to encourage conversation.

Yet where activity at Bridges was open to curious visitors, shades were drawn on the first floor. The overhead warehouse door was down and locked except for the now-familiar delivery truck, and even that was unloaded behind a closed door.

Consumed as she was by Bridges, she couldn't help wondering what the noisy activity on the first floor would produce. But Sam kept their encounters few and far between. He had all but avoided her since the day of their kiss.

"Folks are getting so excited about the new stores," Lacey said, between sips of iced latte. The gleaming new brewing equipment was stationed atop an 1890s saloon bar courtesy of the Carlton brothers. Tara's acquaintance with the pancake moguls was proving to be heaven-sent.

After one glance at Bridges's floor plan, the

twins simultaneously insisted there was another must-have in the barn back home. Hoisting the twelve-foot, marble-topped cabinet up the double-wide flight of stairs was tricky, but who argued with brothers who brought along their very own forklift?

"Excitement is nice as long as it translates into sales," Tara replied, her nose in the user's guide. "All this thing does is make coffee and it's more complicated than the computer we bought to manage the inventory."

"Stop calling it coffee. It's espresso. Coffee is sold at the gas station for seventy-five cents. Espresso costs four times that much and nobody sells it but Bridges." Lacey held her cup aloft with pride.

Tara's throat tightened as she offered up a prayer of gratitude for her dear friend. There were sleepless nights when Tara feared remaining in Beardsly was a mistake. Once the polite outpouring of sympathy ended, few people had seemed particularly glad to see her stay on.

Not that she'd expected a party or anything, but she hadn't anticipated some folks being downright hurtful. Being ignored in the market or not offered a seat in church reminded Tara of her youth when the extroverted locals had mistaken her shyness for arrogance.

To make matters worse, word was out that there was friction between her and Sam. People weren't sure what it was about, but many had made up their minds that Sam was near-perfect. What did that make her?

He courted the college students with a master's skill. They adored his unconventional lifestyle. He was virtually camping in the tiny apartment, going for broke with his business, and seemingly had not a care in the world about the financial outcome. The fact that he had so few material possessions yet seemed so rich in life experience drew students to his door like kids to an ice-cream truck.

"He's like the Pied Piper," Tara muttered.

"Huh?" Lacey scrunched her brow. "I thought we were talking about the new espresso machine."

"I'm sorry." Tara whacked the crown of her friend's head with the small paper manual. "I got a little distracted there for a minute. Okay, I confess, I'm nervous about the opening."

"Why?"

"Has it escaped your notice that folks are treating Sam like a conquering hero while I'm not exactly getting a warm reception?"

Lacey crossed her arms and tilted her head in concentration. "Well, if you think about it, he's an easier fit than you. They don't have to stretch too far to embrace Sam. You, however, always were on the quiet side and you've changed so much since you moved away that they really don't know you."

Tara snorted at the observation. "Oh, right, and Sam's the same today as he was nine years ago."

"Truth be told, yes, he is. Sam may be physically different, but in his heart he wants the same things. An uncomplicated life, respect, friends."

Tara suspected she was the one person in town who saw through the good-old-boy act. Was she also the only one who remembered he had a Master's Degree in Economics? "Please don't tell me he has the hook set in your lip, too?"

"Maybe he does. And maybe you need to dangle a little bait of your own." Lacey swirled the ice in her plastic cup.

Tara slapped the manual on the surface of the bar. "Meaning?"

"Meaning, get to know everybody again. You make zero effort to fit in. For starters, look at yourself." She waggled fingers up and down at her friend's dark apparel.

"I sold you that great outfit and you wore it once the day you bought it. You insist on shrouding your body in long black pants and skirts even in the heat of the summer when everybody else is in shorts."

"That's not fair. I don't tan like everybody else. I'm fish-belly white when you're all brown as cocoa beans."

"And that won't change if you don't get out of those fancy pants and into something short and cool," Lacey insisted.

"There are a couple of very good reasons why I don't dare." Tara held up two fingers. "One, in case you haven't noticed, I've put on about twenty pounds. My thighs are more dimpled than a golf ball. And, two, the glare from my skin is enough to put somebody's eye out. So I'm doing us all a favor and keeping my fancy pants on."

Lacey gulped the last of her latte, crunching ice from the bottom of the cup as she considered her response. "If you'd spent any time reconnecting with the few high-school friends you had, you'd have noticed that none of us look like we did when we were teenagers. And most folks don't care. Appearances may be everything on Madison Avenue, but down on Beardsly Square we like to think it's what's inside that counts."

"You sound like my grandmother," Tara conceded.

"That's because most of our grandmothers tried to teach us the same thing. I know Miss Miriam didn't bring you back here to hurt you. She had to believe you'd figure out how to fit in or she'd have made it easy for you to stay away."

"You think?"

Lacey rounded the bar. "I'm positive." She draped her arm around Tara's shoulders. "So stop worrying about what's wrong with you and let's focus instead on the stuff that's a perfect fit for Beardsly. I'm going to get a pad and pencil from the office and we're going to make a list of things to get you into circulation before the grand opening."

At nine o'clock, Tara flopped faceup across the bed. The motion of the ceiling fan caused the Battenburg lace canopy to billow overhead. Long past being tired, she huffed out a deep sigh of exhaustion. Throbbing quads and biceps cried out from the physical work of hanging wallpaper and installing hardware.

But nothing ached more than her head from the afternoon of brainstorming. Two weeks would be enough if she kept a tight schedule. Watching her time judiciously, she should be able to make all the upcoming events and still wrap up a thousand details at Bridges.

During the years Tara had lived in New York, Lacey Rogers had become an expert listener, the virtual spout of the town's communication funnel. Any information of note passed through Lacey's Closet. As a result, the details of every baby shower, birthday party and Sunday school social were tucked away in her planner.

A few strategic phone calls produced a gaggle of friendly invitations. Tara's life was already a whirlwind of activity, but she was about to be thrust for the first time into the storm surge of Hurricane Beardsly. She prayed her nerves could handle it.

After a cool shower, her damp hair hanging past her shoulders, she slipped one of her grandmother's old patchwork gardening smocks over a pair of baggy shorts and padded down the stairs.

The side-by-side refrigerator yielded bottled water and leftover pizza. The silence of the kitchen was broken by the whir of the huge appliance and her thirsty gulps. Errant drops of the soothing water dribbled down her chin. She wiped them away with the hem of the smock, then lifted her hair to press the chilled bottle to her neck.

The three-tone door chime echoed inside the quiet house. Rolling her eyes at her friend's persistence, Tara plunked the bottle on the countertop, and crossed into the dark foyer.

"Please don't tell me you thought of something else," she called out as she pulled open the massive walnut door.

"As a matter of fact," Sam said, "I *was* thinking of something else. But with you standing there looking like a crazy quilt, I can't remember what it was now."

Chapter Seven

"How did you get here?" Tara demanded, as she ducked behind the door.

"I took College Avenue through the center of town." He pointed toward the business district. "Then I went south on Maple, east on Sycamore and here I am."

"Very funny. I'd love to stay for your whole act but I'm afraid I'm not dressed for company."

"Why, yes, I noticed. But it is nice to see you in something colorful even if the look is a bit *mature* for you." He angled toward the open doorway to get a better look.

She ignored his criticism.

"How did you get here without me hearing you? That infernal machine is loud enough to wake the dead."

"Oh, it's 'that infernal machine' now, is it? The

last time you were on it you said it was 'incredible.'"

She dropped her chin, mouthing a three count, then glanced up. "Do you remember *everything* I say?"

"Don't flatter yourself, Rusty. It's the curse of a good memory. And to answer your question, it appears I pulled up while you were upstairs. I know it's late, but would you mind if I come in?" he asked. "We need to talk about the building."

"I'm ready to collapse. Can't we put this off until tomorrow?"

He shook his head. "Sorry, I'm tied up for the next few days and this can't wait."

Resignation crossed her freshly scrubbed face. Without makeup she was even more lovely. He looked away.

"Count to ten and let yourself inside. I need to change." She ducked out of sight, her light footsteps beating a rhythm on the wooden floor.

The screen door thwacked closed behind him. One step across Miriam Elliott's threshold was a step backward in time.

Dorothy Kennesaw had lost her husband in Vietnam. The monthly Social Security check wasn't much so she made ends meet for herself and Sam by cleaning for the well-to-do. The big house on Sycamore was Thursday's employer. Each week

Sam stepped off the school bus and into a fantasy world.

The little apartment behind the grocery was homey, but Sycamore House was the stuff of his daydreams. Long after he was old enough to be a latchkey kid, he still met his mother on Thursdays at Miss Miriam's. Part of the attraction was the incredible beauty of the home and its contents. He'd studied the rich woods and breathed in the history of the pieces.

But another part, the most important part, was the redheaded girl who waited for him on the steps. At five years old she'd been a giggling shadow. He'd dubbed her Rusty. At eight she'd become a persistent pest. At eleven she was an endearing mass of skinny arms and legs and he was a high school junior with big dreams, a pile of homework and a broken dirt bike.

Rusty became a casualty in the battle for his time.

He hesitated at the carved pocket doors leading to the parlor. From habit, he eased his feet from well-worn boots and set them aside. After several reverent steps on the Persian carpet, he knelt to brush his fingertips across the handwoven silk.

It had taken months of work for an international locator, and twenty thousand dollars, but the same tree-of-life pattern Sam had memorized as a boy now lay before the leather sofa in his private office in Houston.

"Isn't it spectacular?" Tara stood in the door-way, dressed in jeans and a Yankees T-shirt, her damp hair deepened to a thousand autumn colors.

"I researched it for an art-history project and found it's one of a kind."

"Is that so?" he asked.

"Absolutely." She moved to his side, leaning in for a closer inspection. "It's called a tree of life."

"Interesting." He nodded. "But I think there's a possibility you may be wrong about it being one of a kind."

She shook her head, the wet tips of her dark locks whipping across her shoulders. "No, I'm certain of it. I considered specializing in Persians when I went to work at The Heritage."

With an affirming glance at the carpet, he pushed to his feet. "It may take a while, but I'm pretty sure I'll eventually prove you wrong." He offered his hand to shake on the deal.

With a small smile, she clasped his palm with hers. "Fire your best shot."

"Oh, my guns are loaded, Rusty, and I think it's time I had the last laugh." He noted a slight shadow of pain cross her face at the sting of his words and for the first time wished he could take them back.

Stepping away, she dropped his hand. His gaze locked on the fingers she passed through her damp curls. "I'm exhausted. What's the reason for your visit?"

"In a minute." He wouldn't be rushed. He turned, admiring the rich appeal of the furnishings against the backdrop of hand-stamped, sapphire-and-emerald wall coverings and intricate woodwork.

"Would you mind showing me around the place?"

"You've been here a hundred times."

"But not for years. Please?"

She nodded and led the way.

The tour of the main floor ended on the back veranda. He squatted to study the partially restored desk.

She clicked on the porch light and the overhead fan creaked into action. "This is the desk I bought from the Carltons."

He slid a hand from the sturdy foot up the length of one leg, and across the edge of the desktop to rest on the tragically spray-painted surface.

"Do you think you'll be able to get the paint off the leather?" he asked, and glanced up to see her chewing her full lower lip, a familiar and endearing sign of worry.

"The hardware store ordered a special stripper for me by express delivery, so I should know this time tomorrow whether or not the leather will have to be replaced."

"You've done such a fine job with the rest of the piece. It would be a shame to have to use new leather to finish it." He stood and ran his hands across the padded surface. "Worst-case scenario, you could find an old piece of distressed leather for the upholstery."

He backed away to study it again. "I can't wait to see it finished. I bet it'll bring three grand. I'd love to have it myself."

When she didn't respond, he turned to find her leaning against the porch rail, arms folded across her chest, studying him.

"What?" he asked, afraid he'd shown too much interest in the piece.

"You're a conundrum, Sam."

"Excuse me?"

"Everybody believes you're so uncomplicated, back to the basics and all that, but I'm on to you."

"You reckon so?" he challenged.

"As a matter of fact, yes, I do. One minute you're the carefree biker, the next you're the local expert on economic indicators. By day you're a secretive entrepreneur, deliberately hiding behind closed doors, and by night you're a parking-lot philosopher, espousing the simple life."

"And you don't think it's possible to be all those things?"

Tara pushed away from the banister and took several steps closer.

"It's not only possible, in this case I'd say it's probable. And I don't have a problem with it, but a lot of people in this town will when they figure out you've deceived them."

He squirmed beneath the weight of her words. His crouched position became figuratively as well as literally uncomfortable. Rising to his feet relieved the pressure on his knees but did little to reduce the worry building inside. He stared at the plank floor.

She was right.

He was beginning to enjoy his image as the needy beneficiary who seemed to eschew personal possessions in favor of teaching others his altruistic values. When the day came to claim his pound of flesh, would he find the price had become more than even he could afford to pay?

If Tara was already on to him, maybe it was time to cash in before the stakes were too high. Maybe it was time to end the charade.

As he drew a breath to speak, he felt the warm touch of her hand against his bare forearm and shifted his attention from the floor to her fathomless blue eyes.

"Sam, it's okay to admit you haven't made much of yourself since you left Beardsly. People here are happy you've got this second chance to do something with your life. You don't have to keep pretending that you have so little by design. One day you may be able to afford all the things you try to deny you desire."

Sam placed his hand over her soft fingers, gently rubbing the pad of his thumb across her knuckles. He exhaled, grateful he'd held his breath and his confession.

"It's that obvious, huh?"

She nodded. "I'm afraid so, Sam."

"I have to admit, Rusty, some of the things you said are right on target. And you've given the philosopher in me plenty to consider. Now, let me give you something to think about."

He rested his palms atop her shoulders and slid both hands down to her elbows. Gently pulling her to his chest, he wrapped her in a loose embrace and dipped his head to kiss her. His nostrils filled with the essence of the cinnamon scent she wore.

Tara surrendered to the kiss. Her arms slipped around his waist. Surprised by his unplanned action and her unexpected reaction, he loosened his grip. Refusing to accommodate his shift away from her, Tara pulled him once again into the embrace, evidently intent on continuing the kiss.

His mind strained against the jumble of spicy smells. And he realized with a jolt that there was nowhere in the world he'd rather be at that moment.

Heart pounding a fearful cadence, he raised his head and set her an arm's length away.

"So, everybody thinks I'm a failure?" he asked, denying the appealing warmth of the moment.

She gave a negative shake of her head. The drying curls glowed beneath the light above the veranda.

"That's not what I said."

"But it's what you meant." His self-control and matter-of-fact attitude slipped back into place. "Now that I have this chance to 'do something with my life' as you so carefully put it, I don't intend to blow it."

"I know you well enough to believe that's true, Sam."

He stepped away from the glare of the light, into the shadow of the doorway. "Actually, Rusty, you never knew me well at all. But you will."

He opened the door and she preceded him into the kitchen, a room he once knew like the back of his hand. His gaze scanned the glass-fronted cabinets, falling on familiar pottery mugs and earthenware bowls. Little had changed, least of all the know-it-all opinions of some people.

"The insurance on the building needs to be increased to cover the contents."

"I know," she agreed. "I have the forms from the underwriter in my to-do stack." She angled her head toward the oak pedestal table, heavy with file folders and unopened envelopes.

"I don't know about Bridges, but Sam's Cycles needs a half-million in coverage for loss or damage."

She whistled at the amount.

He held out his hand. "Why don't you give me the paperwork so I can handle it?"

"Because it's all still in Grandmother's name. I'll fill everything out and Davis will be happy to notarize the changes for me."

"Davis?" He jumped on her mention of Davis Fairweather, the recently elected county clerk. "Gettin' cozy with a local, huh?" Sam prodded. He had spotted the social-climbing Fairweather on his numerous trips up the stairs of the Elliott Building in recent days.

She shook her head no but the stain in her cheeks said otherwise. Battling the mental image of the up-and-coming politician and Tara Elliott, Sam stalked through the dining room into the foyer.

Feeling like a jealous fool, he flung the front door wide and stomped across the front porch. "See that you take care of that right away. I wouldn't want to be you if the river rises and my bikes aren't insured!" He shouted over his shoulder without a backward glance.

"See you soon, Sam," Tara called, a note of amusement in her voice.

The front door closed with a whoosh, and the dead bolt snapped. Sam lengthened his stride to the end of the walk, muttering as he went.

"So Sam Kennesaw's a failure, huh? They all think they know so much. Well, we'll just see who has the last laugh."

At the edge of the pavement, he stepped down six inches to the gravel drive, all hundred and eighty pounds on his support leg. Pinpoints of pain shot into his foot from the loose gravel walkway. He sat backward onto the step, his eyes squeezed shut in disbelief, as he remembered something important.

His boots.

Chapter Eight

"Welcome back, Sam." Claire Savage placed a toasted bagel on the granite coaster Sam used to protect his walnut Edwardian partner's desk.

"You're my business manager, Claire, not my mother. You don't have to feed me breakfast." He didn't need to glance up from the spreadsheets he studied to know she'd be impeccably dressed, despite the casual workplace. The Harvard Business School graduate was a curious mixture of beauty queen and savvy shark.

"Can I help it if I enjoy a domestic task now and again?" She stepped behind his leather chair and placed her hands atop his shoulders, her strong fingers kneading competently. "You're tense. What secret mission has your muscles in knots?"

"Okay, Claire," Sam tossed his reading glasses on the stack of documents. He swiveled the chair to face her, folded his arms and assessed the former Miss Texas.

"You don't have a domestic bone in your body. What's up?"

She shoved her hands in the pockets of her silk suit and perched on the edge of his credenza.

"Am I that transparent?"

"Like a windshield. So, tell me, what is it?"

"Well, I'm not sure how to put this."

He watched her with a close eye knowing something serious was percolating in her brilliant mind. In the four years he'd known the articulate blonde, he'd never seen her at a loss for words.

"Just shoot straight, like always."

Her straight-shooting had ensured their relationship was strictly professional. Soon after they'd met, she'd told him she limited her dating to Christian men. Since he wasn't sure where he stood with God, Sam was out of the running. She'd become his business manager and shown no interest beyond his financial holdings.

"First, how about telling me where you've been the past month?" she asked.

"I'm sorry I've been so secretive." He paused, letting Claire think he was giving in to her usual probing for information. "But I've been taking care of some legal matters in east Texas."

"Are you being sued, Sam?" She pressed to her feet, brown eyes wide with concern.

"No, it's nothing like that." He motioned for her to sit. "I'm helping out with the estate settlement of a woman my mother worked for when I was a kid."

Her eyes narrowed, piercing him with the stare she reserved for bankers and customers behind in their payments.

"This woman left your mother part of her estate?"

"Not exactly." He waved a hand dismissively. "It's complicated and I don't want to bore you with the details. Suffice it to say I'll need you to continue managing everything a while longer. Would you mind?"

The frown flipped upside down and spread into her best beauty-pageant smile.

"Not at all. Being on site every day has taught me so much more about the business. I'll even admit your charming customers are getting under my skin."

"You just enjoy having those men making fools of themselves over you."

"Well, certainly it's not insulting," she admitted.

Sam knew the guys were awestruck over finding the legendary Claire Savage running the place. She knew it too and was so sure of herself she'd never blush over a compliment the way Tara would.

Tara. The scent of cinnamon drifted through his memory.

Where she was concerned, he was no better behaved than the customers who drooled over Claire.

Every time he'd been near Tara lately he'd done something foolish. He'd kissed her. Twice. And three nights ago he'd walked out of her house in his stocking feet and kept going.

"You're not listening to me, Sam." Claire slapped her palms on the smooth desktop for emphasis.

"Of course I am."

"Then what did I say?" she challenged.

"You said you liked the customers." He faked it.

"Which is part of why I want you to consider selling me half the business."

"What?" He bolted upright in the Windsor chair, certain he'd misunderstood. "Are you crazy?"

"There are more flattering ways to respond to a woman when she's offering to make a significant investment in your business."

"I don't need an investor."

"Then think of me as a partner," she encouraged.

"I don't want a partner, either. I want you to stand in for me for a few weeks. That's all. Enjoy the change of pace, stretch your horizons, meet interesting people and be well paid for your trouble. But don't expect anything more."

"At least tell me you'll think it over, Sam." The determined tilt of her chin told him she hadn't heard a word he'd said.

"Do you understand me, Claire?"

"I always have." She flashed her most beguiling smile.

The intercom interrupted the exchange.

"Claire, Joe Mason is here about the V-Rod and he—"

"I'll be right there," Sam barked into the speaker.

Claire extended her hand, palm outward, signaling for him to keep his seat. "There's no need. Joe and I have been negotiating this sale for a couple of weeks and we're about to close the deal. You get back to your spreadsheets and I'll tell him you send your regards."

Joe Mason, the penny-pinching heavyweight champ, negotiating? The guy owned four top-of-the-line models already and he'd never given a dime more than he had to. Maybe Sam owed Claire more credit than he was willing to admit.

But *not* a share of his business.

Besides, Claire was capable of developing an idea of her own. He wished he could tell her about Bridges but wasn't willing to admit the duplicitous life he'd been living in Beardsly.

He glanced at his watch and imagined Rusty at her desk sipping her late-morning latte. He rubbed the heels of his hands over his eyes.

What had come over him? Checking the time and wondering what she was doing when he should be reviewing his investment portfolio.

"And you have no idea when he plans to return?" Tara asked the construction worker. She was sick to death of talking to a stranger through a six-inch crack in the door. The building inspector was asking questions and she needed Sam's input. This determination of his to keep everything under wraps was wearing thin.

Behind the plate-glass windows hung with dark drapes, saws whirred and hammers banged away day and night. Delivery trucks backed into a darkened warehouse, the overhead doors clanging shut before cargo was revealed. The place was shrouded in secrecy.

By contrast, Bridges was virtually open to the public already. Free samples of espresso were offered to browsers who oohed and aahed over the Elliott Building's second-floor improvements. Tara basked in the excited compliments, almost convinced that staying in Beardsly had been the right decision.

"No, ma'am. I don't know when Sam will be back. He said he had things to check up on and he'd be here directly."

"What does that mean? Directly?" She'd almost forgotten that Texans have a language all their own.

"Well," the carpenter drawled. "That could mean directly after dark or directly after summer. All I can tell you is that if you keep an eye out toward the corner, directly he'll come around it." He smiled a bumpkin smile that didn't fool anybody, least of all Tara.

"I don't suppose you know how to reach him?" It was worth one more try.

"Don't suppose I do." Bumpkin shook his head, raised his hammer in a congenial wave and closed the door.

She dragged herself up the new staircase for the hundredth trip of the day. The reason the second floor had seemed so appealing at one time was a mystery to her now. With calves and thighs groaning against the ascent, she stepped to the landing that positioned customers before the entrance to Bridges.

She'd selected hunter green as the trademark color to carry throughout the store. The deep hue striped soft cushions on comfy Adirondack porch chairs and adorned awnings above the front windows and doorway.

Leaded-glass doors she'd salvaged from the demolition of an old country church had been installed. The thick pine planks and smoky windowpanes hinted at the atmosphere inside where shoppers would find hundreds of books to browse and lasting treasures to buy. She turned the brass knob and stepped into the cool interior, pungent with the smells of fresh paint and coffee beans.

She had a hundred and one details to attend to before the evening's schedule. Back in her office, she moved her stack of to-do envelopes from the top of the desk to the pencil drawer as she checked her planner. She actually looked forward to the string of get-togethers. There was a kitchenware party at six, a golden wedding anniversary celebration at seven thirty and a candlelight prayer vigil for the troops overseas at nine.

She'd be worn out but she'd fall asleep as soon as her head hit the feather pillow, too exhausted to wonder where Sam was or what he was up to.

Sam dropped the day's *Wall Street Journal* on the nightstand beside his bed as he sank down onto the thick mattress. He hooked first one heel and then the other into the wooden jack and pried off his black leather boots.

After a quick shower he slid between the cool, Egyptian cotton sheets and punched the voicemail function of his speakerphone.

"Boss, it's me again. That redhead was by the new shop twice today. I sure hope you make it back up here tomorrow. If I play dumb one more time she's gonna draw back and hit me with that little black purse."

Sam's laughter rang in the spacious master bedroom.

"One last thing," the voice continued, "I got confirmation from two more bike chapters so we're on track for a heck of an opening-day crowd."

The phone clicked off, leaving the room in silence. The evening quiet Sam always preferred had left him anxious and tossing in his king-size bed for the past two nights. The comfort of the custom-built bed no longer appealed compared to the pull-out sofa in his tiny apartment in Beardsly.

He admitted to himself that it was more about familiar background noise than back support. Two months ago he'd have chosen his River Oaks home over any five-star hotel in the country. Tonight he'd rather be with the chattering kids who congregated on the steamy, heat-soaked asphalt parking lot than alone in this hushed, climate-controlled, personal sanctuary.

He stared at the white walls and the tray ceiling above his Danish headboard and considered adding some jewel-toned wallpaper and the vintage look of copper molding overhead. And as long as he was remodeling, he might as well rip up his boring carpet and lay a handsome mesquite floor. He glanced at the modern furnishings and realized they wouldn't suit the new look of his bedroom. What he'd need could only be found at an estate auction.

He squinted as the hundred-watt lightbulb went on over his head. He was unconsciously copying the rooms of Sycamore House. Tara's home.

His insides knotted in an unexpected and unwanted surge of confused feelings. But not for the house. For the woman who lived there.

The revelation robbed him of sleep and by seven he was fueled with black coffee and on the road.

Each mile that brought him closer to Beardsly drew him closer to her. His pulse raced in time with the tires on the pavement when he left the city, the road narrowing to two lanes as he moved deep into the country.

It would be over in a few days. He'd have his moment of revenge. Then he could put it all behind him forever and return to the life he'd built for himself after the Elliott women had yanked the rug out from under him.

His moment of revenge. The thought that had excited him weeks earlier held less appeal today. All the more reason to get on with the plan before it lost all attraction. He'd invested too much time and money in the scheme not to have the last laugh now.

"It's so good of you to come. I know how busy you are with your own big event just a couple of days away." Emily wrapped her arms around Tara and pulled her as close as thirty-eight weeks of pregnancy would allow.

"It's my pleasure." Tara smoothed her hand down a cascade of silky brown hair and patted the girl's thin back. "I'm glad Lacey let me know about your shower."

Tara followed the mother-to-be as she waddled into the fellowship hall where a small group of women waited to share cake and childbirth stories and their secondhand newborn things. Emily had come to Beardsly against her farming family's wishes four years ago as a college freshman. Now, just short of graduation she found herself pregnant and alone with no means to support a child.

"I promised God and my baby that I'd find a way. But from the looks of things—" she smiled around the circle of strength "—he found a way for me."

For the umpteenth time in her life, Tara wondered how her grandmother had found the courage to give up her own precious child. Even more, she was amazed at the faith of her mother in giving Miriam a second chance through the gift of a granddaughter.

They blessed Emily with prayers of good health and lifted their hands in praise and thanksgiving for the new life she carried. Laughter echoed in the church hall as each mother confessed her most embarrassing moment of child-rearing ignorance. Tara pinned a twenty to the money tree and placed a small stack of children's books wrapped in pink-and-blue paper on the gift table.

She admired the confident glow in the eyes of the unwed mother, marveling over the girl's sense of peace in what was surely the most uncertain time of her life. Emily was not fearful about her lack of security. Instead she looked forward to the precious child God was about to entrust to her.

An hour later, Tara cut the engine on the luxury

sedan and took the steps up to the second floor of the Elliott Building. The script letters spelling out her store's name were emblazoned boldly on the canopy above the door. In two days she'd place the open sign in the front window for the first time and welcome customers.

Flipping lights on as she walked through the rooms, she saw the displays of merchandise with fresh eyes. Colorful glassware was creatively back-lit through stained-glass window panes. New computers hummed atop heirloom library tables and stacks of *New York Times* bestsellers were clustered inside apple crates from the flea market.

There was embroidered linen, mismatched silver, a maple hope chest and a brass headboard, all shown to best advantage by strategically recessed lighting. Tara stood in the center of her store and turned slowly, drinking it all in, overwhelmed with pride in her accomplishment.

"Thank you, Gran," she choked on the endearment, "For giving me this chance to come home. I've learned a lot about this town since you've been gone, but I suspect you knew I would." Her grandmother always insisted that roots ran deep and they would eventually pull her back where she belonged. Maybe it was true.

Three sharp raps at the entrance preceded the bell that jangled as the door swung open.

"Anybody home?" Sam called.

Tara cleared her throat. "Over here," she answered.

Sam made his way through the maze of merchandise, stopping every few feet to touch and admire. He nodded approval, his eyebrows arched over wide eyes. "You got some nice stuff here, Rusty."

"I reckon so," she used his favorite phrase. "I see you finally got back."

"Early this morning," he acknowledged, poker-faced, unwilling to share any details.

"How's everything looking downstairs?" She took a few steps toward him.

He puckered his lips and nodded his head. "No complaints. One more day should do it." He shoved his hands into his hip pockets, keeping his distance. "You been lookin' for me?"

"The building inspector came up with a half dozen minor questions during your mysterious disappearance." She waited to see if he'd offer an explanation. He didn't. "As it turned out there was nothing I couldn't handle. So, crisis averted."

"Glad to hear it." He turned to leave. "Well, I'm outta here."

"Sam?"

He rested his hand on the brass doorknob and regarded her with dark eyes that gleamed beneath the overhead lights.

"Good luck on Saturday. I hope it will be a day we'll always remember."

"Oh, you can take that to the bank," he said as he slipped out the door.

With one heavy boot poised above the bottom step, he turned and looked back up at the name on the awning. He was glad it was almost over. He'd had his fun. It was time to end the charade and head back to his real life.

But if that was what he really wanted, why hadn't he slept well the past three nights? Why had he tossed in his bed, missing the small town that was winning his affection and the auburn-haired beauty who was winning his respect along with his heart?

Chapter Nine

Two grandfather clocks on either side of the entrance chimed the half hour. In thirty minutes Bridges would officially be in business. The sweet tones of three violins and a bass cello filled the air as the college orchestra's string quartet tuned up for the morning's event.

Silver clinked against cake plates while Lacey and her volunteer crew laid out the light brunch of quiche, fruit salad and pastries. If the RSVP notes could be counted upon, there would be at least thirty-five hungry visitors when the doors opened.

Tara brushed her hands nervously down the front of her vintage black-lace blouse and demure ankle-length skirt. The many ornamental mirrors decorating the walls confirmed her professional demeanor was flawless but did little to soothe the last-minute fidgets.

Would they come? Had her whirlwind round of baby showers, church potlucks and book-club meetings been enough? If she'd shown up at the campus library one more time she was afraid she'd be arrested for loitering. Tara made a mental check of the list she and Lacey had worked out diligently. Between deliveries at Bridges and short trips to the house on Sycamore for a few hours sleep, she'd done little else for the past two weeks besides reconnect with Beardsly's residents.

She'd barely laid eyes on Sam the day before. She'd drifted off to sleep last night praying away the niggling uneasiness that he was up to something.

"Ms. Elliott, where would you like these Depression-glass goblets?" The doe-eyed female student hired to work the espresso machine had been put to work unpacking last-minute arrivals.

"Those pink facets will sparkle like rubies if you set them on that shelf near the window," Tara replied, gesturing toward the distressed pine cabinet.

"I think that's about everything." Lacey shoved blond curls out of her eyes. "As soon as the girls finish setting up, we'll be ready for customers."

Tara reached for her friend's hands to steady a case of runaway nerves. Lacey bowed her head, tugged Tara close and murmured a prayer.

"Loving Father, I trust you didn't bring Rusty back to us to let her fail. Bless this endeavor, if it's in Your perfect will. Amen."

"Was that necessary?" Tara insisted, huffing out a pent-up breath.

"You know prayer is always necessary."

"I meant the nickname." Tara forced a scowl. "I agree with you on the prayer. I need all the divine intervention I can get today." She ran fingers across the back of her hair to confirm the tight braid was still intact.

"If you want my opinion, I think you should have worn that yellow blouse and left your hair down."

"I'll take that under consideration when we open our Austin branch," Tara teased. "Now, let's check everything one last time. We've got twenty minutes before our guests arrive."

"It *is* a stunning piece, isn't it?" Tara agreed with the married couple who admired the Victorian desk while they sipped free cappuccino. "I handled the restoration myself so I know every inch of it by heart."

"Are you willing to come down on the price?" The woman's voice was hopeful. "It would be perfect in my study."

"Not anytime soon." Tara palmed her business card to the husband. "But check back with me in a week. I doubt it'll still be here, but if it is I might reconsider."

As she drifted among her guests, the soothing melody from the quartet and the murmur of conversation filled the room. Judging from the first hour's turnout, Bridges's grand opening was going to be a rousing success.

Then the rumble began.

At first it was low and far away, like the hum of an eighteen-wheeler passing through town. Then it grew closer and louder, a persistent roll of thunder spoiling the quiet morning. And finally it became a roar that pierced the peaceful atmosphere and rattled the gleaming windows.

With voices overcome by the demanding sound, conversation dwindled and heads turned. Worse still, potential customers discarded their cups and plates and headed for the entrance to investigate the source of the sound. Tara didn't have to follow their lead to know who she'd find behind the disturbance.

Sam Kennesaw.

In the lead, Sam guided the pack of bikers past the college administration building and library, right up Main Street toward the Elliott Building. The colorful swarm, numbering close to two hundred, filled the air with a chrome-plated symphony. Decked out in their leather and denim finery, they cruised the streets of Beardsly two by two. Couples rode, men in front with wives and girlfriends behind, but women on their own bikes were in strong representation.

Sam couldn't hold back the smile he felt from his chin to his eyebrows. Beardsly had never witnessed such a parade, and his gut wrenched with desire for the town's approval.

The bikers' approach was the signal for the dark shades over the first-floor windows to be rolled up, exposing the interior of the shop to daylight for the first time. The double glass doors were swept wide and the tarp above the entrance was tugged to the pavement revealing the expensive neon sign. Sam's Cycles was open for business.

Red cones were set up at either end of the street to block all but bike traffic that streamed into the re-stricted area and parked at angles forming an im-promptu bike show. Engines were cut, leaving the patrons of Bridges and passersby with a slight ring-ing in their ears. The echo was soon replaced by classic Elvis and Jerry Lee Lewis broadcast from Sam's state-of-the-art sound system.

As the tower clock struck noon, a catering truck backed a huge portable barbecue pit into the re-served space. The massive lid was raised to expose tender racks of baby back ribs, roasted chickens and mouthwatering grilled burgers. Tubs of baked beans and potato salad along with gallons of sweet iced tea covered the serving tables that flanked the pit.

Sam shook hands and accepted good-luck claps on the back as folks lined up to enjoy the hearty feast. He couldn't resist an occasional glance up the exterior stairway. With all the excitement out front, very few signs of life remained on the second floor. Just as he'd planned.

With an oddly troubled heart, he realized his carefully executed mission was accomplished.

He made his way past the throng of well-wishers into the interior of the shop. The black-and-white checkerboard tile floor, flashy orange walls and neon-rimmed showroom windows were a classic setting for the pristine bikes, display cabinets filled with after-market parts and racks of T-shirts. At this moment he'd expected to be filled with smug pride. Instead he felt a lump of guilt the size of Dallas settling into the pit of his stomach.

"I suppose you're pleased with yourself." Tara stood with arms crossed just inside the door to his small office.

"Well, good afternoon, Rusty." He let his gaze sweep over her, approving for once of the black lace that contrasted with her beautiful fair skin. "May I offer you something to eat?"

"You know very well that I have plenty of food upstairs."

He caught the quiver in her chin as she jutted it a fraction higher to cover her distress.

"Why would I know anything about your plans? You never made any effort to discuss them with me," he challenged.

"I left a dozen messages for you this week. I didn't have a phone number to reach you and nobody seemed to know where you were." Her cheeks began to color with emotion.

"I've been back for two days," he insisted.

"Yes, I know, sneaking past your 'guards' in the alley in the morning and leaving at who knows what hour under the cover of night." Her eyes gleamed with unshed tears. "You did this on purpose just to spoil my plans."

"Kinda like you spoiled mine?"

She dropped her arms to her sides, her shoulders and chin sagging in defeat. "I should have seen this coming. I knew all along you were only doing this to get even with me."

"That's where you're wrong," he continued the lie. "I'm in it for the chance to rebuild my life in this community and I intend to be successful. If you're not, that's your own fault. And if I enjoy a little payback along the way, I'll consider it icing on the cake."

"Well—" she turned to go "—I'll leave you to savor your dessert."

The thick auburn braid trailed down the row of covered buttons, her creamy skin peeking demurely through the heavy lace.

Sam closed the door behind her and flopped into his desk chair. It wasn't supposed to be like this. On his day of triumph, he should be handing out his Houston business cards, flaunting his success. Instead, he was perpetuating the simplistic persona he'd inhabited for over a month. He steepled his fingers and rested his chin against them to reevaluate his plan.

"I've been such a fool," Tara insisted. She soaked up the dribble of tears, careful not to smear her mascara. She and Lacey were pressed together in Bridges's small restroom.

"Why? Because you trusted him to do the right thing? And because you did everything possible to make amends with the folks here?" Lacey patted her friend's back. "Honey, that's not foolish, that's honorable."

"Yeah, well, honorable is a luxury I can't afford right now. Everything I have is at stake and my customers are out in the street eating barbecue courtesy of Sam's Cycles."

She gave a final noisy blow and dropped her tissue into the trash. With Lacey close behind, Tara returned to the cashier's counter.

"Look at this," she ordered. Both heads bent over the register receipts. "We've barely made enough to cover the coffee grounds and the day's revenue has already peaked," she fumed.

"I don't know what makes you say a thing like that," a voice called from the doorway. "We're not the Rockefellers but last time I checked my bank statement I could still afford a book and a cup of decaf." Ward Carlton entered the room, a sight for sore eyes.

Tara hurried to hug her new friend, determined not to burst into fresh tears.

"Where's Walter?" she asked, looking past Ward for his twin.

"Oh, he'll be on up in a minute. He's downstairs with our womenfolk. They couldn't resist takin' a gander at those fancy bikes. Walter thinks he might like to have him one."

Ward strolled toward the saloon bar turned coffee counter. "Didn't I tell you this old piece was perfect for this spot?" He slid a gnarled hand across the polished surface. "She cleaned up real well." He turned and winked at Tara

"With a lot of help from me," she countered.

"Well, God helps those that help themselves, so I'd say you're due for a little interest on your investment." He put an arm around her shoulders and pulled her close. "Don't you worry, little girl. You're gonna be just fine."

She dropped her gaze to the floor and cleared her throat.

"So," he spoke to the young lady behind the counter. "What does an old man have to do to get a fancy cup of coffee around here?"

"Make mine a double shot. And we'll take some of that quiche before it's all gone." Walter and two ladies crossed the floor to join them.

"Excellent suggestion," Lacey answered from the buffet table, as she readied a plate for each of the newcomers.

Ward made introductions as the quartet returned from their break and launched into a lively Irish jig. The twins' silver-haired wives, clutching their plates and designer bags, began to circle the room admiring the unique furnishings and wide variety of books and collectibles.

Tara was refilling a pastry tray when the door opened to admit a dozen women outfitted in boots, tight jeans and T-shirts and a wild assortment of leather accessories. The primly dressed Carlton wives turned to stare at the group as they drifted into the room.

"Welcome to Bridges. May I serve you ladies some fresh fruit?" Tara was quick to offer.

"Oh, would you? I'd love something besides barbecue and potato salad for a change," one admitted. "Don't Texans know there's life apart from beef and spuds?"

"Please, help yourselves," Lacey encouraged.

The women swarmed the buffet table in response, cooing their approval of the meal.

And as they ate, they shopped.

As night fell, a country and western band in the gazebo on the square struck up a rousing Texas two-step. Tiny white lights tucked among the branches twinkled by the thousands as couples gathered around to listen to them play. Spirits in the small town were higher than they'd been in years, thanks to one man.

Sam Kennesaw.

He admired the neon sign above his door. *Sam's Cycles* was scripted in his very own handwriting. It wasn't how he'd intended to make his mark on Beardsly, but it was as rewarding as his name above a classroom doorway any day.

At that moment he made a decision. He was going to stay. For a little while longer, anyway.

He glanced at his watch, knowing his chance to atone was ticking away. Bridges would close any minute and Tara would slip out the handicapped entrance to her car on the side street. He took the wide staircase two steps at a time, his heavy boots announcing his arrival.

"Come on in and browse. We'll be closing soon but there's still cappuccino if you're interested," Tara called from her crouched position behind the bar.

"I'm interested, but not in coffee," he drawled. "I've got something to say."

Her head popped into view, azure eyes wide with surprise over the identity of her late visitor. Then the eyes narrowed with suspicion.

"If you've come to gloat, don't bother." She rounded the counter, drying her hands on a white cotton apron. "We managed to rally despite your best efforts to spoil my grand opening."

"Is that so?" he asked.

"And, believe it or not, some of my best clients turned out to be your biker friends."

"Hmm," he fingered a large sold tag on the Victorian desk. "No wonder my sales were low today. The women had the checkbooks in their purses and they were up here all afternoon."

Tara stood at his elbow, took the tag from his hand and flipped it to reveal the price.

"Three bills? You got three grand on a twenty-five-dollar investment?" He whistled his approval. "I'm impressed, Rusty."

"Are you?" She seemed reluctant to believe his compliment, keeping her eyes fixed on the paper tag.

"Absolutely. In fact," he glanced around with a nod of approval, "I'm impressed with your whole place. You've done quite a job of assessing what would sell and pulling your plan together in a hurry."

"Well, thanks." Her eyes were still downcast. "Is that what you came to say?"

"No, I came to say I'm proud of you." He drew his index finger in a soft line beneath her chin so she'd meet his gaze. It wasn't the apology she'd expected, but it would have to do. "You've taken this mission your grandmother gave us very seriously and I'm gonna do everything I can to keep up my end of the bargain."

She stared at him, the look in her eyes saying she didn't quite believe what she was hearing.

She extended her right hand. "Would you care to shake so we can call it a day?"

He took her hand, warm and soft and small in his own.

The urge to spend more time with her was strong and the party atmosphere outside offered just the excuse he needed.

"I have a better idea. Do you remember the day I taught you to pitch horseshoes?"

She arched an eyebrow, suspicious of the sudden change of subject. "Of course, but I haven't held a horseshoe in years and I'm out of practice."

"You were a natural." He squeezed her hand as emotions he didn't yet want to acknowledge squeezed his heart. "Come on, Rusty. Let's go show these folks how to toss a ringer."

Chapter Ten

"**I**f I didn't know better I'd swear the two of you were an item," Lacey chided.

"Then it's lucky for me you *do* know better," Tara reminded her matchmaking friend. "Sam was only being polite. He came up to congratulate me on my opening day and as long as we were on our way out the door, we played a few rounds of horseshoes."

Lacey scrunched her brow and rolled her eyes heavenward in a display of disbelief. "Tara, you know people are talking."

Tara agreed there was reason this morning for tongues to wag. Sam had looked rugged in his denim shirt, jeans and boots. Women spent shameful amounts of money trying to achieve the luxurious hair he swept off his forehead with an air of nonchalance. Sam was gorgeous and he knew it.

He was sending Tara mixed signals on purpose, trying to lower her guard so he could twist the knife some more. And with each tenderness the devastation afterward was worse. She should end it today and never let him get close to her again. But the plain truth was she didn't want to.

She decided to turn the tables and take advantage of every private moment she could steal with Sam. Anything was better than nothing at all.

Her grandmother had been right. It had taken very little for the feelings to flood Tara's parched soul.

She still loved him. There, the admission was made and it stung like a fresh paper cut.

"They'll find something else to talk about by lunchtime." With a wave of her hand Tara hoped to dismiss the assertion that she and Sam were interesting fodder for the town gossip mill.

"You may be right," Lacey agreed. "After seeing staff cuts at the college on the front page of the *Herald* this morning, folks will have something else to worry about."

With endowments and donations no longer sufficient to support the rising payroll and equipment costs, the downsizing of the faculty loomed as a budget-reduction measure. Making matters worse, a tuition increase had been a threat for years and there was little doubt it was coming next. With the town's economy already in a slump, job losses at the school and higher fees for the students would drive more people than ever out of Beardsly.

"You reminded me of something important." Tara thumped her palm against her forehead. "Miss Frieda called from the campus bookstore this morning to say there's a meeting tonight in the Mount Zion fellowship hall to discuss the impact of the layoffs on the town."

"Lacey's Closet closes before Bridges so I'll get there first and save us a seat up front."

"That would be great."

"Well," Lacey fished her keys from her oversize shoulder bag, "I've gotta get going. My place ran on autopilot yesterday so I have a lot of catching up to do."

The two hugged, exchanging comforting pats on the back.

"I can't tell you how much I appreciate your help for the past few weeks, especially yesterday. I'd never have managed everything without you," Tara whispered.

Lacey gave her head a negative shake. "It would have taken you a little longer, but you'd have figured it all out on your own. But that's what friends are for, Rusty."

"Still…"

"Hush," Lacey insisted. "All you have to do is open your heart to this town again and the folks will all be there for you."

"As usual, you're right," Tara agreed. "And tonight it's my turn to be there for them. See you at seven o'clock."

"And wear those capri pants," Lacey shouted on her way out the door.

Left alone with a list of chores and her thoughts, Tara considered the timing of this economic crisis and the vulnerability of her business. Diversification beyond the original plan was a must. A new business with high-end products would never survive unless clients could be lured from larger cities. She settled on the ladder-back chair behind the register to scribble ideas on a notepad.

Sam may have intended his display of biker friends as a distraction, but Tara had turned it to her advantage by making sales and capturing some valuable information. She flipped open the guest register and reviewed the names and addresses supplied by the shoppers.

Houston, Dallas, Austin, Tyler and more. The guest book confirmed that the opening-day visitors were from all over the eastern part of the state. Tara would have a special-event mailer designed, printed and at the post office by close of business.

Her mailing list would grow with each customer referral. She penciled notes on hosting a variety of book clubs and study groups. She'd invite her circle of New York associates to visit the quaint Texas town as guest speakers. Entertaining lectures on everything from publishing to public auctions would become synonymous with Bridges.

She'd tout the unique atmosphere and hospitality of her shop for hosting private events. The occasional crank of a bike from downstairs could present a problem, but after Sam's gruff compliment the night before, he might be more inclined to cooperate.

"Sam." Tara whispered the name as she relaxed her shoulders against the back of the chair.

Sam was even more vulnerable than she was. At least she had an avenue to pay off her business debt if worst came to worst, but Sam appeared to be doing everything on credit.

And questionable credit at that.

"I won't be able to stay in school if tuition goes up," the young man complained during his daily stop by Sam's Cycles. "My folks can hardly afford to send me as it is."

"Have you considered giving up that new gas-guzzling truck of yours to cut back on expenses, Alan?" Sam spoke up from his position on the floor where he was adding a chrome cover to a used sports model.

"No." The kid shoved fisted hands into his baggy jeans pockets. "I couldn't live without my truck."

"That's hogwash, and you know it. There are used cars in the paper every day that would cut your payments and save you lots of money on gas and insurance." Sam fixed the kid with a practiced stare. "The more stuff you have, the more stuff you need. Try life with a little less of it and you'll find it's a lot easier."

Alan chewed the toothpick that protruded from his lips and seemed to chew as well on the downsizing concept. "You know my folks will want to drug-test me when I volunteer to get rid of the truck."

"Once they get over the shock of it, I promise you'll find yourselves agreeing for the first time in years."

"Thanks, Sam."

Sam squinted against the sunshine pouring through the glass doors as the kid headed for his next class, a heavy backpack slung over his shoulder. The advice Sam gave was sound, but he felt the smallest twinge of hypocrisy. There was a time when he'd practiced what he'd just preached, even if it had been a while.

He shook off the uncomfortable feeling and returned to his task. As he steadied the bike with one hand and turned the crescent wrench with the other, his thoughts drifted to Frieda's early-morning call. The challenge of rallying the local business owners for the sake of the school had such hometown appeal. He was downright excited to be invited to participate.

His two-day revenge trip was stretching into two months with no end in sight, and he'd grown fond of the locals. Especially the students. Word of his Spartan-living philosophy had spread among the young male population and they sought him out in increasingly larger numbers. At first it was to get a look at one of the few custom bikes in the area. Then it was for academic and career guidance. Now they stopped by his tiny apartment at the drop of a hat for advice on everything from the price of gas to the girls they liked.

When talk turned to women, Sam surprised even himself when he became the spokesperson for reason and restraint. As odd as it seemed, the biker's conservative views endeared him all the more to students and parents alike. Small-town values slipped back over his life like a favorite sweater, old-fashioned and comforting.

With reluctance Sam realized the things he valued had never changed, even though the direction of his fortunes had taken a major turn. When the folks who'd opened their hearts to him found out about his wealth, and he was forced to leave again, he knew it would be much harder the second time.

The fellowship hall was packed. Tara made her way through the crowded room, smiling into worried faces and touching tense shoulders as she passed.

Pastor Ryan asked everyone to take a seat. She spotted Lacey motioning to join her near the front. Tara edged toward the rows of chairs, stopping to greet a group of women she recognized from Emily's baby shower.

Tara sank into a folding metal chair next to her friend, immediately aware of the man seated in the row before them. His thick mane was subdued beneath a baseball cap. A few dark curls escaped, contrasting with the white T-shirt stretched tightly across his muscular shoulders.

"Hey, Sam." Lacey gave his hair a tug. "Anybody sitting in those two seats?"

He turned with an easy smile for Lacey and patted the chair beside him. "Saved this one for you." His eyes flickered to Tara. "I reckon your friend can take the other."

Lacey jostled Tara across the packed front row and into the seat right beside Sam. As the meeting began, Sam sat with his feet planted wide and his elbows resting on his knees, leaning forward and giving his full attention to the pastor.

Worse than a schoolgirl, Tara couldn't think beyond the solid form pressed so near.

She nervously crossed and uncrossed her legs several times. Then she covered her mouth with her hand to clear her throat as if that would clear away her thoughts. Sam glanced over his shoulder and gave her squirming a disapproving glare.

"Thank you all for coming out on such short notice. It's suppertime and I hear stomachs rumbling, so we'll try to keep it short." There was a ripple of agreeable laughter.

"As you all read in the *Herald* this morning, the college is about to announce some staff and curriculum downsizing. You probably wonder why I'm the one talking to you and not Dean Grant. Well, he's spent most of the day meeting with the City Council to get a proposed tax increase moved up to the general election in November."

The group groaned its displeasure at the news.

"I know how you feel. Money's tight everywhere and nobody wants to see tax increases. That's why Dean Grant is making personal phone calls to every member of our alumni who may be capable of increasing their giving." The pastor paused for enthusiastic cheers then held up his hands to silence the sidebar conversations that broke out across the room.

"Beardsly College is our largest employer and has offered a fine education to our young people for over a hundred years. The faculty and staff have always been here for us, and now it's our turn."

"You're not fixin' to pass the plate, are you, Pastor?" a man shouted. The pastor laughed along with the others and shook his head.

"I wish it was that simple. No, our goal tonight is to put together a team of merchants to develop a major fund-raising campaign with the proceeds going to the college." He glanced down to the front row. "Sam and Tara, I know this is putting you both on the spot, but you did such a splendid job with your grand openings. Would you two be willing to head this committee and manage this fund-raiser?"

Before either could respond, a burst of applause approved the nomination.

Sam stood, turned to face the crowd and extended his hand toward Tara. The gripping fear of standing before a crowd was immediate and intense. There was no choice in the matter. She placed her palm in his, praying he wouldn't notice hers was sweating already.

Sam tugged Tara to her feet and pulled her behind him to the podium.

"Thank you for the encouragement," he spoke into the microphone. "I hope we're worthy of your vote of confidence."

He took a step to the side. "And now my partner, Tara Elliott, will tell you how we're going to raise a million dollars."

Chapter Eleven

"A million dollars! Are you crazy?"

"I didn't mean it in the literal sense."

"Then why did you say it?" Tara demanded.

Sam enjoyed the way her auburn eyebrows drew together when she was annoyed. At the moment she was a grown-up version of the little girl who'd scowled over math homework and science projects.

"We need to raise a small fortune and it might as well be a million as a fraction of that at this point."

"Exactly how are *we* supposed to do that?" She motioned with her index finger back and forth between the two of them.

Tara and Sam sat in a booth at Ruthie's Kitchen, the daily specials on the table between them all but forgotten.

"We're meeting tomorrow night at your house as

you so eloquently suggested." He held up both hands to defend himself against the fork she brandished.

Overcome by nerves, Tara had sputtered in front of the podium. She finally drafted people for a core team and recommended they sleep on it and come to Sycamore House prepared with ideas the following night.

She stabbed into her meat loaf with the fork as he continued. "We'll have each committee member present their individual ideas and then vote on them. We'll plot a timeline and some rough revenue projections and discuss it with Dean Grant on Thursday. Between our efforts and what he's been able to accomplish, I hope we can offset any budget shortfalls for the rest of the fiscal year."

"Then what? The town can't be expected to step in every time the college needs money."

"No, but I'm confident the alumni will come through and the Board of Regents will find other areas to reduce cost without cutting jobs."

"Meanwhile, we pray," Tara said, matter-of-factly.

Sam was silent, pushing green peas around his plate.

"You still pray, don't you, Sam?"

"No," he muttered.

"Why not?" she pressed.

He met her gaze. "I just don't feel the need anymore."

She stared hard, as if trying to see into his very soul.

"When you left Beardsly did you leave behind your faith, too?"

He focused on the gold flecks in her blue eyes as he considered the question.

"No, I still remember what I learned in Sunday school. I simply don't need it anymore." He tore off a bite of yeast roll to keep his hands busy and stuffed it in his mouth.

Her eyes narrowed at the blunt words. She wasn't going to let it go.

"Let me ask you something, Sam."

He pushed his plate away. "I'd rather we got back to the subject of the fund-raiser."

"Just let me give you one thing to think about." She covered his hand with hers to hold his attention.

"What if you lived all your life accepting the sacrifices your mother made for you, but never thanked her for it? And what if you'd never bothered to share your heart with her because you thought being close to your mama was something you didn't need anymore?"

"Get to the point." He tugged his hand free to check his watch.

"If you don't share your heart with God, how can you have a relationship with Him and know what He wants for your life?"

"I know what *I* want for my life and that's all that

matters. A long time ago I tried doing things—" he crooked his fingers indicating quotation marks "—the 'Christian' way. It didn't work out, so I'm living life on my own terms, now."

"I didn't get what I hoped for, either, Sam. But I still trust that in His time, God will give me what He feels I need."

He arched one eyebrow and stared pointedly into her face. "With your grandma's money you didn't have to worry about whether or not God would come through for you. You've always had everything you could possibly need."

Color suffused her throat and fingers of crimson crept up her neck. Sam marveled at the speed with which her creamy, fair skin became a mottled mask of obvious discomfort. She didn't close her eyes and start that silly breathing. Instead, she stared him down, her eyes bright with the threat of tears.

"I said, 'I didn't get what I *hoped* for.' There's an obvious difference and, since your memory is so good, there's no need for me to embarrass myself by elaborating."

Recalling her tender declaration of love all those years ago, he felt a stab of regret over the hand fate had dealt him. A split second later he shook off the nostalgia. He'd become so adept at playing the pauper he'd almost convinced himself it was true.

In fact, from a financial standpoint, he was a hundred times more successful, thanks to the upset that sent him away from Beardsly. His life in Houston lacked nothing of material value. He lived in comfort in a fashionable River Oaks home with a state-of-the-art, six-car garage to showcase his car and bike collection.

So he didn't have what he'd once hoped for, either. He certainly had much more than he needed. And here he was, needling Tara to the point of tears.

And for what? Amusement? More revenge?

No. He was past those things. He was doing it out of self-pity. The very idea sickened him.

Her hand still rested on the tabletop where he'd shrugged it off moments earlier. He slipped one palm beneath hers and cupped it with his other hand, rubbing his warmth into her cool fingers.

"You're right."

"On which count?" She stared down at their hands and let out a long slow breath as if to expel some of her distress.

"Both. What I once hoped for is not what I got, but I have almost everything I need."

She lifted moist eyes and squeezed his hand. "Almost?"

As he studied the full lips curved into a sympathetic smile, he felt a rush of compassion. And something else he was pretty sure was...love.

For Tara Elliott.

* * *

Tara stared at the lace canopy over her four-poster bed and counted the rings in the intricate pattern the way an insomniac counts sheep.

She had a lot of nerve lecturing Sam about his faith. Her own belief that God intended Sam to be her husband was the very thing that had flipped both their lives upside down. She should keep her mouth shut on the subject and enjoy their occasional moments of closeness. But a small voice inside told her to speak out again when she got the chance. Sam knew the truth and he would return to the roots of his faith in God's timing, she felt certain of it.

She replayed their evening together in her mind. Tonight he'd held her hand between his, his face wearing a small grin that hinted at his perfect smile. At that moment she'd struggled against the need to lean forward and kiss him, right there in Ruthie's Kitchen.

Grandmother was either hiding her eyes or leaping for joy in Heaven. With each day that passed, Tara suspected the latter was true. Miriam had devised this plan so she could smile from eternity at her final earthly accomplishment.

So many critical issues loomed in Tara's mind. This was no time to be overwhelmed by a schoolgirl crush. She had to get a grip. The store needed her. The college needed her. The town needed her. If only Sam did too.

Hadn't he looked her right in the eye and told her he had almost everything he wanted? If his cycle shop continued to do well he'd have financial security. All the things he'd hoped for were within his grasp. When he could afford the life he'd always wanted, would he still be satisfied by a small east Texas town?

An unexpected excitement flowed through Sycamore House. Instead of feeling the weight of the town's problems on their shoulders, the committee members' spirits were buoyed by the creative ideas each had come to share. Every chair around the oak dining-room table was occupied and the dessert plates had been cleared away.

"Ward, would you like to get us started?" Tara asked with her pen poised over a notepad.

"Be glad to," Ward Carlton spoke up. "We've made a pretty good living flipping flapjacks."

The understatement drew chuckles from the small group.

"I think I should stick with what I know and volunteer some kind of flapjack-eatin' contest or an all-you-can-eat flapjack week with the profits going to the college fund."

Sam nodded agreement. "Great idea, Ward. Lacey, how about you?"

Lacey leaned forward with a gleam in her eye. "I want to put on a designer-collection runway show. It won't be fashion week in Milan, but we could sell a lot of tickets and have fun at the same time. I can get the clothes on loan from the merchandise mart in Dallas and we can have the women of Beardsly as our models."

"You can count on my wife," Ward said. "She's always looking for an excuse to buy new shoes. I swear the woman's got more pairs than Imelda Marcos."

"We have two excellent ideas so far. How about you, Sam?" Tara asked.

"I'd like to supply an anniversary-edition model to be auctioned off to the highest bidder."

"What?" the table chorused.

Sam held up his hands as if he'd expected the confused reaction. "I provide the bike at cost, the auction reimburses Sam's Cycles and the profit goes to the college fund."

"What happens if nobody can afford to bid that much?" Ward put words to everybody's thoughts.

"Leave it to me. I have friends who can come up with the money if we don't get a local bidder willing to go that high."

Tara shivered as a crop of goose bumps prickled her arms. Sam's frequent references to his "friends" with money concerned her more each day.

Wade Latimer cleared his throat and pushed tortoiseshell glasses up his nose, signaling he was ready to speak.

"It so happens that I am prepared to coordinate a silent auction. After forty years of practicing law in Texas, I have hundreds of professional friends and acquaintances who could be convinced to donate as well as bid on items for a worthy cause. It would be my pleasure to wring every last dollar out of their rich pockets. And I for one think auctioning off Sam's bike would be a spectacular finish."

"You're not gonna charge us two hundred dollars an hour for your services, are you, Latimer?" Ward slapped his friend on the back.

"Don't give him any ideas," Sam quipped. "How about you, Tara?"

The full attention of his dove-gray eyes was like a caress in the crowded room. She returned his smile, proud to share her contribution.

"I would like to propose that we do our own version of the *Antiques Roadshow*. I'm qualified to evaluate a number of collectibles and I've already contacted one of the partners from The Heritage and he's willing to spend a weekend in Beardsly acting as a guest appraiser. We can charge a small fee and let people bring their items for appraisal. We could even tape it and run it on the East Texas Cable Channel afterward."

Excitement erupted around the table as each idea was discussed for merit and financial potential. They were close to a frustrating impasse when Sam joined Tara in the kitchen to make fresh coffee.

"Sam, I appreciate your generous offer but I have to admit I'm worried about these friends of yours. We can't afford to have any shady dealings involved with a college fund-raiser.

He dumped two more scoops of grounds into the filter, turned to face her and leaned against the tile counter. He shook his head at her comment and grinned. Mesmerized by the vision of his lazy smile, she lost interest in filling the glass pot under the tap. Water overflowed the pot and splashed in the sink, bringing a sparkle to Sam's eyes. She filled the coffeemaker and dried her hands.

"Can I ask you a question, Sam?"

"If it's about my friends, no, you can't. You're just going to have to trust my judgment."

"It's something else. Something personal."

He stepped closer, inclined his head toward her and waited.

She hesitated, hoping he wouldn't be offended. "When did you get your teeth fixed?"

"Oh, that. Actually, not too long after I got my first job in Houston. They had good dental coverage so I invested in orthodontic work."

"I don't think I'd ever have worn braces if the choice had been mine," she insisted, remembering her early teens with a mouth full of metal.

"Back then I'd have given about anything to trade places with you," he said.

"Are you serious?"

"You better believe it. I'd run into you and your girlfriends at the theater and you'd be complaining about not being able to eat popcorn or caramels and I'd promise myself that one day I'd have that problem."

"And what handsome results you have for keeping that promise," she complimented him.

He glanced toward the kitchen doorway and stepped even closer. He lowered his mouth to her ear. "I'm glad you approve," he whispered.

"Sam, I have guests." She placed her palm against his chest and gave a weak push.

"And I have a proposal."

"Excuse me?" Her eyes flew wide.

"Not that kind of proposal." He chuckled ruefully. "Come with me." He lifted the tray and took a step to the side allowing her to lead the way.

When everyone was seated Sam explained his plan.

"All our suggestions are creative and doable. The problem is that no single plan will generate the kind of cash we need. But if we managed to combine everything, in a festival-style weekend, we could do it all. We might even be able to turn this into an annual event."

"We could call it Texas Treasure Days, to honor our state champion Pirates baseball team and try to fill a big treasure chest up with money," Lacey enthused. "This has huge potential, Sam."

Tara listened with pride as each committee member praised Sam for his plan. As she watched him drawing out a timeline on his notepad and making to-do lists, she was reminded of the young teaching assistant who had stood before the class discussing and exploring economic concepts.

There was no doubt about it. Sam was in his element.

Chapter Twelve

"How can we ever repay Miss Frieda for coordinating the publicity?" Tara asked.

"The woman missed her calling. She's worked night and day for the past two weeks and the results of her efforts are spectacular."

Tara and Lacey edged across the crowded lot as a throng of visitors parked their cars on the already steamy asphalt and prepared to descend on the Beardsly College campus for the day's festivities.

"She's still got fifty cents of the first dollar the campus bookstore ever made," Lacey pointed out. "We should have known she'd take our meager budget and turn it into a windfall."

Getting the word out on Texas Treasure Days had been a full-time job since the date had been locked in. With fourteen days to plan and execute the event, each member of the team had spun into a mad rush of activity. The town pulled together to cooperate in a manner that could only be compared to their response to the tornado of '38. The twister that had leveled Main Street had nothing on the Texas Treasure crew.

Word spread throughout the interstate network by truckers who stopped at Flapjack Heaven and left with a stack of event fliers tucked in the bright yellow to-go bags. Churches got the word out through prayer chains, and prayer warriors came from hundreds of miles away to be firsthand witnesses to God's generosity.

Metropolitan papers carried the heartwarming story of the town that pulled together to prevent teacher layoffs and tuition increases. Radio and television stations sent reporters and camera crews across the state to interview the Treasure Team for Sunday inserts and human-interest pages.

The students built the Texas Treasure Web site, updating it as the schedule of events, celebrity visitors and auction items grew. The town hummed with excited activity. Residents invited family members they hadn't seen in years to come for a visit. And they all showed up. With every room within ten miles of Beardsly rented for the weekend, historic homes opened their doors and became temporary bed-and-breakfasts.

Sycamore House was no exception. The Heritage Auction Company in New York City would be well represented by the owner's son, Ethan Beckham, and his assistant. The confirmed playboy had taken up residence in the spacious downstairs master suite. From the moment he stepped across the threshold into the historic home and began to examine Miriam Elliott's antique collection, his appraiser's nature had been kicked into overdrive. Tara knew it was all he could do not to take out his calculator and begin tapping in figures.

"Oh my stars." Lacey's eyes flew wide as they rounded the administration building and got their first look at the line forming outside the cafeteria. Dozens of people lugging prized possessions were already waiting with hopeful expressions on their faces.

"I *knew* this was going to a draw a nice crowd," Tara said, awed by the early turnout. "But I didn't expect them to start arriving for a while yet."

"These are probably the same folks who turn up at garage sales at dawn."

"The early birds." Tara nodded agreement. "Fortunately, we're all set and Ethan has consumed his weight in double-shot espresso so he's chomping at the bit to get to work."

"You have to be at the auditorium at six sharp to get dressed for the fashion show," Lacey reminded her friend.

"Like I could forget? I can't believe that with everything else I have to worry about, I let you talk me into that, too." Tara attempted a stern glare.

"Oh, relax. It's gonna be fun. All you have to do is walk out on the stage, pause and turn at each of the marks, and then exit behind the curtain. You'll be a natural."

"I'll probably be a klutz and everybody will demand their money back. You have me in something black, right?"

"Gotta run. See you at six." Lacey made a quick getaway.

"She *better* have me in something black," Tara muttered.

Sam backed the hundredth-anniversary classic off the trailer and walked it up the path to the gymnasium. He was tempted to crank it up for special effect, but Miss Frieda's media blitz had been so successful that working to draw attention was not an issue this morning. Cars began filling up the narrow streets well before the events were expected to begin.

The items listed on the Web site for silent auction had daring first-timers and seasoned bidders out in droves. Latimer had come through with his claim that he had more favors to call in than Johnny Cochran. Everything from Nolan Ryan's autographed cleats to a Caribbean cruise was listed in the catalog, still warm from the printers. True to his word, Latimer had showcased the hard-to-find bike as the grand finale, the must-have item of the auction. Sam positioned it beneath the spotlight set to show off the custom paint job and stood back to admire his contribution.

Leaving nothing to chance, he'd planted a few associates in the crowd to drive up the bid. So what if he ended up buying back his own property? It would be more fun than donating the money outright and his cover would be protected.

"You've outdone yourself, Latimer," Sam clapped the lawyer on the shoulder to show his gratitude.

"Well, thank you." Latimer's eyes glowed behind his horn-rimmed glasses. "I haven't had the opportunity to work a cause like this in a long time. It's been exciting watching this event come together in two weeks. You've certainly played a key role in making this happen, Sam."

"I don't know about that," Sam shrugged off the accolade. "I got a few permits pushed through with the promise to teach a bike-safety course this fall."

"Don't try to brush it off. Everybody on the committee knows how hard you and Tara have worked to coordinate all the weekend events and we won't forget it."

At the mention of Tara's name, Sam couldn't help but smile over the long line outside the campus cafeteria. Everything that could be balanced on a hand truck seemed poised and ready for its moment before the appraiser. Television stations from

Houston and Dallas had sent crews on the outside chance that something of unusual value was discovered.

"You have things under control in here, so I'm going to go check on the rest of the team." Sam gave Latimer the infamous salute and headed for the exit.

Inside the cafeteria, volunteers categorized items and directed owners to the proper stations. Originally, Tara and her friend from New York were to be the only appraisers. But once word of the event hit the airwaves, there were volunteers from other auction houses eager to participate in the town benefit.

It was a good thing, because two professionals, no matter how well-rounded and efficient, could never have serviced the unexpected crowd. There was no doubt about it. At twenty dollars a pop, Tara's brainchild was going to contribute handsomely to the Texas Treasure fund.

Even in the noisy room, packed with artwork, furnishings and excited visitors, Sam spotted the sleek auburn braid trailing down the back of a somber jacket. On a day when most folks battled the heat with shorts and tank tops, she was dressed in her black *uniform*. Probably to impress the rich guy and his elderly assistant who were freeloading at Sycamore House.

Sam had to admit, even in the heat, the clingy dark fabric was flattering, making the flashes of fair skin at her neck and wrists magnetically appealing. Watching her now from afar, admiring her quiet confidence, he was intrigued by the emotions she stirred in him.

In the two very long weeks since he'd confronted his feelings for Tara, he'd refused to examine the personal revelation too closely. A great deal of water had run under that bridge and he was certain she'd never risk her heart with him again. As if sensing his gaze, Rusty turned and stared him down. She was not a shy kid anymore. Making it on her own in New York City had given her the bold self-assurance she'd always lacked. And now she was so confident in her faith, something he admired and almost envied.

Tara's heart pounded beneath her lightweight, silk-knit jacket. In recent weeks Sam had locked eyes with her many times in that way of his that made her pray for much more than this cat and mouse game. He'd switched his tactic from controlled anger to manipulative interest, but she knew it was still about revenge.

Sam was drawing out his payback for as long as he could but she was enjoying the rare moments of one-sided intensity. Resisting his attention would be wise, but knowing the probable outcome she chose memories for the future over good sense at the present.

"Who's the guy?" Ethan interrupted her thoughts.

"What guy?" She feigned innocence.

He pointed his number-two pencil in Sam's direction. "Bad boy over there with the dark hair that needs cutting. Bet he owns a motorcycle."

Tara burst into laughter at the astute assessment. Ethan's years of evaluating auction items gave him a sixth sense about people as well as their possessions. He used it to great advantage with the women.

"Oh, you're just jealous because he *has* hair," she pointed out to her prematurely balding employer.

"Don't remind me and stop trying to distract me. Who is he?"

Sam ended his brief conversation with a young man in the line who was carrying a weathered guitar case, and headed straight for Tara.

"Never mind. I'll find out who my competition is for myself," Ethan said as he stood to greet the new arrival.

"Good morning, Sam." Tara smiled to cover the butterflies swirling in her stomach. "Allow me to introduce my New York employer, Ethan Beckham. Ethan, Sam Kennesaw."

"Ah, yes. Sam's Cycles. It all makes sense now," he said with a knowing glint in his eyes.

She adjusted her jacket to cover the motion that sent a pointed elbow into his side. Evidently, he got the message.

"You must be the donor of the anniversary-edition bike that's listed in the auction catalog." The two men shook hands as Ethan inclined his head toward Tara. "When this redheaded tyrant allows me a short lunch break, I intend to grab one of those famous Texas barbecue sandwiches and make a pass through the auction hall."

"Please do. And leave your name on several of the bid sheets while you're there. We're grateful for the donation of your time, but we'd prefer to keep some of your money to remember you by."

"It will be my pleasure," Ethan assured Sam before resuming his assessment of a Revolutionary War musket.

"Got a minute?" Without waiting for her reply, Sam stepped away from the table and Ethan's interested ears.

"In case you weren't aware of it, I have about a hundred people waiting for me." Tara motioned toward the crowd.

"Sorry, I wanted to tell you I noticed you neglected to add Sycamore House to the historic site tour and gourmet meal package. So, I penciled you in myself."

For the second time in five minutes, Tara rammed her elbow into a man's ribs. "There was no neglect involved. I don't want to participate," she insisted.

"Why not?" Sam rubbed the spot where she'd gouged him.

"Because I can't cook! I'll poison somebody," she wailed the admission. "I can hardly warm soup in the microwave. I get carryout from Ruthie's Kitchen almost every night." Perturbed, she stamped a foot. "Sam Kennesaw, you better fix this." She drew back to deliver another blow to his ribs, but he jumped out of the way.

"Okay, okay, I'll think of something, but I can't remove the listing because there's a bid already."

"You think?" She needed convincing.

"I saw it with my own eyes."

Her agitation abated. The idea that somebody would pay money for a tour of the house and a home-cooked meal was somewhat flattering. Maybe she'd get out her grandmother's recipe books and try a few dishes.

"Did you recognize the name?"

"Sure did."

"Well?" She waited. "Who's the unsuspecting victim?"

"Me."

As the day wore on, cash boxes overflowed with sales receipts and the giant treasure chest filled with contributions. The flapjack breakfast ended when the batter ran out, a phenomenon the Carlton brothers had not seen in forty years of selling pancakes.

With the women in the community battling

amongst themselves to model the latest styles, there was standing room only for the fashion show. The silent auction generated lively competition among the bidders, driving prices higher than expected. The arts and crafts fair on the lawn of the library and the barbecue cook-off in the student parking lot enjoyed a steady stream of traffic.

But the big surprise of the day was Beardsly's version of the *Antiques Roadshow*. At five-thirty the line of participants still filled the sidewalk that wrapped around the building.

"Are you sure you don't mind doing this again tomorrow?" Tara asked. The turnout was so enthusiastic that all the appraisers had agreed to stay on another day.

"We can't send these folks away, not when they've dragged hope chests and grandfather clocks all over the countryside. Anybody willing to come back tomorrow will get an appraisal."

She gave Ethan a quick hug, then dropped her arms self-consciously. "I don't know how I'll ever repay you for your help."

"Well, you can start by telling me whether or not you plan to come back to work. You know we can't hold your job open forever."

There it was. She'd known the subject was bound to come up. She'd worked hard for her position at The Heritage and she had a home and friends in New York. Yet, as much as she loved the excitement of the city, she was becoming content with the quiet of the country and the easy pace of her hometown. Her life was full of purpose and friendship. As soon as Bridges turned a profit she'd be able put another part-timer to work.

As a tribute to her grandmother, she'd started the process of registering Sycamore House as an historical landmark, and she was feeling at home at Mount Zion Church. The Bible study group she sponsored met at Bridges twice a week. Tara was growing right along with the students as they studied the Word of God together.

And there was Sam. He had attended church with her the past two weeks but she had no idea where they were headed. More than likely in separate directions, but at the moment she wasn't willing to risk what little time they had left together. She was determined to make the most of the opportunity her grandmother had wanted for her and Sam. If things worked out it would be worth the wait. If not, it was never part of God's plan for their lives and she could accept that.

"I have a lot going on here right now, Ethan, and the store is not quite on its feet yet. I suppose I could get everything running smoothly and then turn it over to a manager. As long as I spend holidays and vacations in Beardsly, I think I can juggle everything. Can you wait another week for my answer?"

"I'm sure Dad will agree to that. You know he's fond of you, Tara. We all are," he narrowed his eyes. "We've never considered allowing anyone outside the family to be a senior associate, but your name is on the list for the upcoming board meeting. If you're back by then you might get the promotion you've been campaigning for since the day you walked through our doors."

One of the mantel clocks waiting to be appraised chimed six times.

"I've gotta go. If I'm late, Lacey will kill me."

"Could you convince your lovely friend to focus some of that aggression on me instead?" Ethan asked with a mischievous grin.

Chapter Thirteen

"I can't wear *that*." Tara shook her head, vehemently objecting when she saw her name pinned to the mannequin draped in a fringed jacket and matching slacks.

"Why not? It's black, just like you ordered." Lacey pressed her lips into a tight line as if she was holding in a snicker.

"But it's *leather*. I only wear leather on my feet."

"Great, because I got matching boots." Lacey set a pair of chunky-heeled boots below the mannequin so the outfit was complete.

The two women stood back and surveyed the effect. "I understand your reluctance but this ensemble is straight out of a magazine."

"By any chance was it *Biker Weekly*?"

"Be a sport, Rusty. It happened to come in your size and you'll be incredible in it. I intentionally re-stricted you to this one outfit in the finale so you wouldn't have to rush around during the show like a chicken with your head cut off." Lacey massaged her friend's shoulders. "You can sit backstage, put up your feet, have a soda and relax. You must be whipped from that crowd today. Hey, I hear y'all did so well that you're gonna do more appraisals tomorrow."

"Don't try to change the subject," Tara shrugged off Lacey's hands. "You waited until the last minute so I couldn't do anything but cooperate."

"Okay, so maybe I did," Lacey admitted her guilt. "It won't kill you to spend ten minutes outside of your comfort zone. Then if you end up back in that stuffy job in New York you'll at least have one exciting thing to tell your grandchildren."

She nudged her friend and twisted her face in a pleading expressing. "Pleeease?" Lacey cajoled.

Tara threw up her hands in surrender. "Oh, all right. But if I fall off those boots and break my leg, you have to promise to peel that leather off and get me back into my business suit before the ambulance gets here."

From the back of the darkened auditorium, Sam enjoyed the parade of local beauties as they sashayed across the stage in the latest designer finery. Husbands cheered as wives who hadn't shown more than their ankles in years, strutted the makeshift catwalk in trendy dresses, silk stockings and fancy heels.

Lacey had chosen a tasteful array of fashions with a few surprising numbers thrown in to keep the applause flowing. The cheers and whistles emboldened the models who were otherwise quiet school-teachers and shy grocery clerks. Feeling as beautiful as they looked, the women posed and twirled and blew kisses to the enthusiastic audience.

Cued by Lacey, Sam slipped out the side exit where his borrowed truck and trailer were parked. He let down the tailgate without a sound and backed the high-performance classic down to the pavement.

Lacey rapped on the dressing-room door. "Three minutes. Break a leg."

"Very funny," Tara muttered as she stuffed her feet into the clunky heeled boots. "How in the world do the kids wear these things without doing permanent damage to their arches?" She'd avoided the mirror until now, but couldn't resist one glimpse at the finished product. She stepped before the full-length reflection and gasped at the daring stranger who stared back.

The kid-leather jacket was fringed across the shoulders and down the length of the sleeves. It snapped perfectly around her waist, quite unlike her suit jackets. The matching leather pants felt unfamiliarly snug.

"Exactly what I needed. Something to accentuate the body part I've been trying to hide since the day I got here."

The door handle rattled and Tara jumped away from the mirror.

"Let's have a look," Lacey insisted from the other side of the door.

Tara yanked the worn handle and swung the door wide. "I'm going to kill you!"

"Tara Jean Elliott, you look amazing." Her smile incredulous, Lacey circled her friend slowly. "This turned out even better than I planned."

"Ah ha! Just as I thought. You did this on purpose."

"It's for your own good. And so is this." Lacey slid the elastic band off the long braid and shook it free. "Check it out." She marched her friend to the mirror, fluffed the cascade of auburn waves and stepped aside.

Tara shook her head to free the remaining curls and, in a bold move, flipped a long strand in front of her shoulder. Even she had to admit the woman in the mirror had gobs of appeal.

The track of contemporary jazz that had served as the background music for the show suddenly segued to a loud rock song.

"Come on," Lacey yelled above the sound track. "That's your cue." She grabbed Tara by the hand, dragged her to the middle of the stage and then abandoned her in the darkness. Through a crack in the heavy curtains Tara could see the crowd clapping in response to the driving beat.

The loud song was soon overcome by a thunderous roar from the opposite side of the stage as a motorcycle revved to life. Like a silent-screen heroine tied to the railroad tracks, Tara squeezed her eyes shut against the oncoming force she was helpless to stop. The curtains parted with a whoosh of air, her eyes flew wide and the audience cheered its approval.

She was transfixed, rooted to the wood floor, afraid to acknowledge the black monster growling in the wings. The rider revved the engine to a fever pitch, popped the clutch and, to Tara's horror, executed a perfect wheelie across the stage before her.

The crowd leapt to its feet, singing, clapping and yelling for more. Though the rider's face was hidden from view there was no doubt as to his identity. There was also no doubt Sam Kennesaw was smiling like the Cheshire Cat behind the dark visor. Tara mentally added a second name to her short homicide list.

The front wheel of the bike dropped to the ground, Sam expertly swung around and roared to a stop at Tara's side. She grabbed the gloved hand he extended, threw her leg over the bike, wrapped her arms around his waist and squeezed hard enough to make his eyeballs pop.

Deaf from the roar of the bike, the music and the crowd, she held tight as they made a turn around the circumference of the stage with a daring run out onto the ramp that encircled the orchestra pit. Once more at center stage, she slid off the leather seat, strode through the three models' marks executing a turn at each, brazenly fluffing her hair and winking at the crowd.

She had no intention of getting back on the bike, but Sam seemed to have other plans. She ignored his outstretched hand, and he responded with a low menacing growl of the engine. She dusted off her hands with a gesture of being finished with the foolishness and the engine roared louder.

Determined to have the last laugh, she grabbed the handlebars, imitated Sam's infamous salute and led bike and rider out of sight.

"That was quite a show." Offstage, Sam ran his fingers through his hair, wishing he could do the same to Tara's unruly mane. She was stunning in the biker ensemble, but then he'd known she would be when he'd had Claire send it from the Houston office.

"Did you have anything to do with this?" Tara demanded.

He gave her a cheeky smile and she rolled her eyes heavenward. "Forget I asked."

"You guys were awesome!" Lacey squealed as

she threw her arms around the pair for a group hug. "We couldn't have done a better job if we'd choreographed what you two ad-libbed. You're lucky I didn't make you go back for an encore."

"And you're lucky I didn't faint from fear." Tara tried to sound angry but the mirth dancing in her friend's eyes was contagious. "Okay." She smiled. "I'll admit it. You two set me up to do something I'd never have agreed to on my own."

"And?" Lacey cajoled.

"And…I enjoyed it. It was great fun."

"There's a lot more where that came from, so let's get over to the auction. The highest bidders will be announced at nine o'clock with the party starting right afterward."

"Give me a minute to change," Tara said as she turned toward the dressing room.

"Or you could keep that on," Sam encouraged.

"Not on your life."

"He's right you know," Lacey agreed. "There's no point in hiding that great figure under a tunic any longer. The whole town knows there's a streak of daredevil in you as wide as the Gulf of Mexico."

Tara glanced down at the sleek, soft leather and remembered the woman in the mirror. It was nice to play "dress-up" but she was more bookworm than biker chick these days and there was no shame in that.

"Maybe some other time," she said wistfully.

"I'll hold you to that," Sam answered with a wink.

Pleased with the clean lines of the white cotton slacks and powder-blue silk shirt she'd stashed in her duffel, Tara slipped into open-toed pumps and secured her hair in a knot with two lacquered chopsticks.

The crowd made its way back to the gym for the results of the silent auction. One final time, the locals and visitors made the rounds of the dozens of donated items, fingers crossed for the winning bid. Wade Latimer surveyed the tally sheets, his eyes bulging behind his lenses. If the look on his practiced poker face could be trusted then they'd far exceeded their expectations with the auction.

"Who won dinner at Sycamore House?" Tara pressed in for a peek. Latimer pulled the results to his chest with a pointed "Ahem" and raised eyebrows.

"You can wait like everybody else, young lady."

"Since I haven't been called a 'young lady' in years I'll take that as a compliment, grab a frozen drink and do as you suggest."

Positioned in the doorway that drew a slight breeze from the overhead fan, she sipped a fruit smoothie, savoring the cool treat. "Mmm," she murmured to herself as the sweet icy drink slid up the straw.

"Hey, beautiful," Sam whispered into her ear.

She angled her head to see into his smoky eyes.

"You seem to be just about everywhere I turn today," she mused. "Any chance that's intentional?"

"Could be," he admitted.

"May I interest you in an official date?"

His eyes widened at the suggestion, the smoke deepening to slate. "What did you have in mind?" he asked.

"You free Thursday night?"

"As a matter of fact, I am."

"Perfect." She smiled with smug satisfaction. "My Bible study group meets at Bridges at eight. We'll be expecting you."

"Excuse me," the striking blonde apologized. She smiled at Tara and Sam, then edged through the doorway and drifted into the crowded room. Tara was alert to the immediate change in Sam. His smile vanished, he straightened and distanced himself a step as his gaze continued to follow the blonde.

She was a stunning woman. Tall and willowy with sleek ivory hair. Just the type that made Tara feel like a fireplug by comparison.

"Somebody you know?"

"She seemed familiar, but most beauty queens do after a while." Nice recovery, but Tara wasn't fooled for a moment.

"How do you know she's a beauty queen?"

"Just a guess." He craned his neck to see what was happening at the awards table. Tara mirrored the tilt of his head and noted Wade Latimer was mounting the steps to the raised platform. "I need to keep my eye on the bike," Sam made an excuse.

"Sure, I'm happy to stand here alone," she said to herself. He'd already left.

"So *this* is where you've been keeping yourself, Sam." Claire Savage was careful to keep her voice down and maintain her distance. At least he had that to be grateful for. She admired the soon-to-be-awarded bike while she surreptitiously quizzed him. "When I noticed an anniversary bike was being donated to this shindig by a local dealer I thought I'd better come check out our east Texas competition. What a surprise to find out you're the Sam behind Sam's Cycles."

"Knock it off, Claire," Sam hissed. "Nothing surprises you. You wouldn't drive two hundred and twenty-five miles without doing your homework first. So what did you hope to accomplish by showing up in Beardsly?"

"I might ask you the same thing? You've been hiding out here for almost three months and it looks like you're settling in."

"I am not," he insisted. "I'm taking care of some temporary business and then I'll be back in Houston."

"All evidence points to the contrary, Sam. I visited your showroom before I made it to the fundraiser. I hear from the local folks that you're living in an apartment near the campus and they think you're fitting right back in to the community again. One of them even told me they were so proud that you were finally getting your act together and making something of yourself." She hid a smile behind her manicured hand.

Sam hung his head, embarrassed. Claire might find his small-town ruse amusing, but Tara would see no humor in the circumstances. His short-term plan for revenge had become a grand scheme to win back everything he'd lost nine years ago.

And now that he had it all within his grasp, he knew it could slip away like a wave on the sand. A cold chill slithered through his nervous system. It was something he couldn't identify.

Yes, he could. It was fear.

Claire dropped to one knee behind the bike to examine the chrome wheels, her face hidden from prying eyes. "Whatever's going on with you, Sam, I encourage you to study and pray about it. It's obvious you're at a crossroads in your life and you won't find peace in your decision unless God's word is part of the process."

What was it with the women in his life forever trying to drag God into everything? But Sam had to admit that his recent visits to Mount Zion Church had been driven by his need for answers.

Claire stood, all five feet ten inches of her, and once again heads turned.

"Can I see you to your car before it gets any later?"

"I can take a hint." She smiled her former Miss Texas best. "Don't bother. When you drive a '67 pink Mustang into a small town, people naturally find a place for you to park and then stand around keeping an eye on it for you. I'm sure I'll be fine."

"It was nice meeting you, Sam." Claire held out her hand. Sam clasped her palm and cupped her hand between his, glad for her friendship.

"The pleasure was all mine."

The auctioneer's gavel banged to signal that the winning bid on the Cottonwood Estate package was final. For an offer of $175 the winner was entitled to a steak dinner on the back patio of the famous plantation house and a night in the master suite.

"The Sycamore House is our final dinner prize of the night. It was a last-minute entry and, believe it or not, has earned the single biggest payoff with only one bid," Latimer teased the crowd to stir up attention. He'd been masterful at creating a buzz over each prize to keep the folks excited and make the winners feel special. "Seems this guy wants to sample Tara Elliott's cooking something awful. Let's hope the dinner isn't something awful." Laughter at the bad pun rippled across the room.

From the moment Sycamore House was mentioned Tara's skin suffused with heat. No deep breathing could hold the rush of color from her face and there was no way to escape and pray until her pulse slowed.

"For a bid of *one thousand dollars...*" Latimer paused for dramatic effect, "the prize goes to Sam Kennesaw!"

As Sam made his way through the crowd to accept the hastily prepared gift certificate, Tara felt the color drain from her face faster than it had rushed there. Sam didn't have the money for such a foolish gesture. She'd have burned him dinner for free if he'd asked.

He seemed bent on giving away what little money and possessions he had, to prove they meant nothing to him. But Tara suspected there was more to Sam than met the eye. She saw the way he appreciated the fine things in her grandmother's home. She'd seen it all her life. He longed for the treasures he would never have. His Spartan life was a cover and the cover was wearing thin.

"Can I help it if I'd like to have one meal in that house that doesn't take place in the kitchen?" Sam asked as they strolled together toward the outdoor grandstand.

His downcast eyes prevented her from guessing the true meaning behind his question. Was he making light of the exorbitant price that he couldn't afford or was he telling her he'd always felt inferior in her home? Either explanation was an issue that had to be resolved if there was any chance for their relationship to progress.

The long days of managing Bridges, planning the fund-raiser and then lying awake trying to figure out Sam's motives were exhausting. With her leave from The Heritage coming to an end it was time to "fish or cut bait" as Ward Carlton would say. She couldn't straddle the fence any longer.

Sam had one more week to show his true colors and then she'd decide her future based on facts and not emotions. She trusted God for the strength and peace to face the outcome.

"We could have flown to New York and ordered the finest dinner they have to offer and not spent a thousand dollars," she admonished. "Sam, what were you thinking? You're trying to get a new business off the ground and you can't afford to donate profits that don't exist. At least that's the way it is for me so I presume you're in the same boat."

"You don't need to worry about my finances," he tried to reassure her.

"I can't help it. My grandmother's crazy scheme got you into this and I'll feel partly responsible if you fail and end up worse off than before."

"You don't have to be afraid I'm going to fail. I have friends—"

"Your *friends* are exactly why I'm scared," Tara interrupted. She lowered her voice as they approached an area congested with revelers who waited for the live music to begin. "If they decide to 'call in their markers,' or however those people put it, you could be in big trouble. Sam, I'm terribly concerned about you," she poured out her fears.

"Have I told you you're beautiful when you're in a dither?"

The country band kicked off the night's entertainment with a lively duel between fiddle and banjo. Sam captured Tara's hand and pulled her to his side. The twinkle in his eyes implied he had little care at the moment for financial worries. The soft kiss he pressed to the top of her head confirmed it.

Chapter Fourteen

"I spoke to Dad," Ethan said the next morning over breakfast. "We can wait another week for your decision but you'll have to be back in the office in ten days if you're going to stay with the firm. The fall schedule is locked in and we'll need you to work the estate sales."

The gray-haired woman who was Ethan's assistant passed him some local honey for his toast as he sweetened the deal. "The commissions on those sales will be huge. You'd have no problem affording a manager to run your little country store and you'd have this home for getaways."

Tara tried to focus on the serious nature of their conversation, but she couldn't stop the flashbacks to the night before. The happy spark in Sam's eyes, the gleam of white teeth when he smiled, the feel of his hand holding hers possessively.

She wasn't misreading him. He cared. She was certain of it. But she also understood that time and circumstances had him guarding his heart from her.

"Tara?" Ethan tapped his butter knife on the edge of the Wedgwood plate. "Are you listening to me?"

"I'm sorry." She returned full attention to her guest. "I'm worn out from yesterday, as I'm sure you must be."

She placed her hand over his wrist and smiled her gratitude. "I can't thank you enough for making this trip and sticking around today for more appraisals."

He dismissed her comment with a wave. "It's my job and it got me out of that city heat for the weekend." He looked out the bay window at the backyard, awash with color from hearty summer blossoms. "I see why you love this place. It's a piece of history and your grandmother's things are incredible. I won't mind staying here another night. Besides," he paused to take a bite from his toast. "I had to stick around to see my bike loaded and on its way to Manhattan."

"I still can't believe you bid on a motorcycle." She chuckled behind her hand.

"Not just any motorcycle. A hundredth-anniversary *Heritage Springer*. Come on," he insisted. "That bike was meant for me."

"What in the world are you going to do with it? If you ride that thing in the city you'll be a statistic inside of a week," she teased.

"I sold the '55 Bird at a nice profit. That leaves an empty bay in the garage in Westhampton. I may never ride it but it'll be a nice conversation piece while the value appreciates."

"Is everything about profit with you, Ethan?"

He chewed his last bite of bacon and squinted into the sunshine while he thought it over. "When the family business is all about turning grandma's old trinkets into somebody's new treasure, I suppose everything is about profit." He peered at her as if for the first time. "Do you suddenly have a problem with that?"

"No." She shook her head. "And forgive me if I sounded critical. Your family has been incredibly generous to me. I adore the business and, if you'll still have me, I may be back at my desk next month."

Her gaze fell to the Irish linen tablecloth that had been her grandmother's favorite. She fingered the hand-sewn lace trim. "It's just that since I opened Bridges to help out the community, that's become more important than turning a personal profit. You think that's foolish, don't you?"

He reached across the corner of the table, and raised her chin so their eyes met. "I think you've inherited a philanthropic gene from your grandmother. This town is very fortunate to have you." He winked. "And so is Sam Kennesaw."

The regulars at Bridges had come to expect an occasional minor explosion from downstairs as bikes backfired and sputtered through the alley exit. On Thursday Tara's nerves were shot from wondering whether or not Sam would show for the evening's Bible class. With each *bang!* beneath her feet she jumped in agitation. She'd spilled more espresso than she'd sold.

Sam had been extraordinarily busy since Texas Treasure Days, a situation she suspected was by design. She'd made it clear during several conversations that she wanted a Christ-centered relationship one day. If Sam had any expectations of their friendship progressing further, he had to make more of an effort to reconnect with his faith. By dodging her, he was dodging God.

"There's such a nice breeze this evening. Why don't we use the ceiling fans instead of the air-conditioning?" Lacey suggested as they pulled chairs into a circle.

"Great idea," Tara agreed. "We have frozen yogurt with toppings for dessert to keep us cool. Why don't you prop the door open so latecomers will feel welcome."

She considered calling downstairs to remind Sam of her invitation, but this had to be his choice.

The study group was a diverse cross section of the small community. Curious students who sought answers and confirmation of their faith brought their friends. Housewives who needed a break from the kids came for an uplifting escape. Ward Carlton often dropped by with a truck driver in need of some fellowship.

There was always excited chatter with faith at the center of the discussion. Tonight's gang seemed ready to relate the struggles of Christ and his apostles two thousand years ago to modern experiences.

"We're on page twenty of the workbook. Our study tonight is on Luke, Chapter 5, as Jesus calls Peter to become a fisher of men." Tara referred to her leader's guide. She'd battled her lifelong fear of speaking before a group and accepted the teaching role. The detailed curriculum made simple work of leading an important discussion.

"I know you've all heard this story since you were little kids." She glanced pointedly at a couple of college sophomores. "And for some of you that was last week." They chuckled at her running joke of feeling old at twenty-eight.

"So let's take a snapshot from a different perspective tonight." She laid aside her workbook, closed her eyes for a moment of silent prayer and then leaned forward with hands clasped on her lap. "Imagine this. Peter fished all night long. He didn't catch a thing, so he won't get paid. He's bone-tired, his bank account is empty and his wife is waiting at home for his check so she can buy school clothes for the kids. But before weary, smelly Peter can go home and break the bad news, he has to clean his nets.

"There's a crowd of people on the shore and, of course, he wonders what's going on. His brother Andrew has been raving about this charismatic teacher named Jesus and it turns out the guy's right there at the dock. While Peter's cleaning up, he can't help overhearing the rabbi who boldly asks if he can sit in one of the fishing boats. For some reason, Peter's moved to stop what he's doing and accommodate the request. When Jesus finishes speaking, he turns to Peter and tells him to drop his nets back into the deep and prepare for a catch."

Tara glanced around the circle. "If you were Peter, how would you have reacted?"

After several fishing puns they settled into earnest discussion.

"I'd probably have argued with the guy," one young man admitted. "If my dad asks me to get out of bed early on a Saturday morning when I'm whipped after a long week, there's gonna be a battle."

"That's understandable," Tara sympathized. "Peter may have felt the same way. He wanted to go home to bed and here's this stranger telling him what to do."

"But Peter never argued with Christ," Lacey reminded. "Why do you think that was?"

"Maybe he was too tired," another student quipped.

Tara laughed along with the group. "Or maybe

in listening, Peter recognized Christ's authority. Think of this…the minute the boats began to sink under the weight of the catch, Peter fell at Jesus's feet and cried out, 'Lord, I am a sinful man!'"

"If his boat was sinking why wasn't he crying for help?" A newcomer appeared confused. "That would be the logical thing to do."

"But there was nothing logical about that day or that situation for Peter. Just as the thief on the cross recognized the divinity of Christ, Peter had the same revelation. And at the moment of knowing he was in the presence of perfection, he realized his own sinful nature."

Tara paused, allowing time for the words to sink in, to let Peter's experience become real and not just a story from a child's picture book.

"Why would the Son of God reveal himself to a fisherman?" a young girl named Sandy asked.

"Good question. You'd think Jesus would go to the politicians and high priests who could accomplish something with the news that the promised Messiah had finally come. Instead, He chose to reveal Himself to tax collectors, servants, prostitutes and thieves. Common people. Sinners. And He continued to choose common men to be His apostles and carry His mission throughout the world.

"It's no different today," Tara continued. "He comes to common people, even in our sin, asking us to work with Him to continue His mission."

"It's hard to get your arms around that concept," Lacey said. "But the fact is that each of us means so much to God that He will never give up on us. And when we seek God's kingdom we witness His response to us in so many obvious ways that we wonder how we missed it for so long."

"Or why we tried to ignore it." Sara, a mother of three preschoolers admitted as she dabbed at the corner of her eye.

"What do you mean, Sara?" Lacey encouraged.

"I knew from the day my first son was born that God was calling me closer. Jim didn't want to go to church so I stayed away, too. By the time all three kids were here, God's voice was so loud and so constant I couldn't escape it. As blessed as I was there was a hole in my life and only He could fill it," she spoke through her tears. "I want my kids to experience God's love the same way I do. I want them to grow up in that love and my constant prayer is that one day Jim will know it, too."

"It would be nice if God would snap His fingers and make everybody obey Him," Sandy said.

Many of the older people in the group smiled at the notion they'd all shared in their lives. Ward spoke up. "Maybe so, but God doesn't work that way. He's a gentleman. He wants us of our own free will and no other way. If Peter had decided to go on to the house that morning, Jesus probably would have let him go. But Peter answered the call and his work to carry out Christ's mission has lasted for two thousand years. That's quite a legacy for a fisherman when most of us just want a ten-pound bass to hang on the wall."

Over laughter and more fishing puns the young mother dried her eyes and encouraged the college students to seek Christian partners *before* marriage. The topic splintered into several conversations as the room fell into its usual practice of breaking into small groups for more intense discussion.

Tara stepped behind the counter where she emptied small baskets of pungent grounds and refilled them. Soon the aroma of fresh espresso wafted through the store. Lacey rounded the bar with a spark of excitement in her eyes.

"What are you up to?" Tara quizzed her friend.

"You mean, what is Sam up to?" Lacey smiled.

Tara lowered her voice and grasped Lacey's hand. "Don't play games. What are you talking about?"

Lacey angled her head toward the door, still standing wide to allow the night breeze inside. "It's getting dark so I was going to close the door to keep the mosquitoes out. Sam is sitting on the landing in one of your Adirondack chairs."

He leaned back against the cushions striped in Bridges' trademark green and sucked in a deep breath. Sam was glad he'd paused outside the door before taking the plunge into the Bible study group.

A half hour earlier, he'd climbed the steps in his sneakers, intentionally keeping his presence unknown since he still wasn't sure he'd go inside. He wasn't sure he belonged in there. What if God had given up on him?

His heart pounded harder with each step closer to the top. He wasn't winded from the climb, that wasn't it. He was growing accustomed to the way his pulse raced when he was around Tara and that wasn't it, either. This peculiar heartbeat was more like anxiety over being confronted with something he'd rather not face.

The inviting Adirondack was all the distraction he'd needed. He'd eased down into the comfortable chair, where he was able to overhear the conversation flowing through the open door. He hadn't meant to eavesdrop for so long, but once they got started he found himself caught between a rock and a hard place, scared to go inside and join in, but afraid to walk back down the steps and miss something important.

To his very core he felt he was meant to be in that chair at that moment hearing those words. It was creepy to admit, but there was no getting around it. The discussion of God's calling being something you can't ignore, no matter how many distractions or blessings there are in life, had hit home.

The small voice Sam thought of as his conscience had been silent for years. It wasn't that he'd done anything to be ashamed of, in fact, he was quite proud of his life. But he wasn't doing the things he knew in his heart that he should. Being back in Beardsly was an awakening for the voice. It pestered him during solitary times in the shop and it nagged him at night in his tiny apartment when he tried to sleep. It even attacked him on the bike when the rumble of the engine should be loud enough to cover a small voice.

And right now the only thing louder than the voice was the pounding of his heart. In Ward's easy way of breaking things down to the basics, he had put it simply. God is a gentleman who wants us of our own free will and no other way. Until Sam reaffirmed that decision for his life, the voice was going to give him a fit.

For the first time in many years, he closed his eyes to send up a brief prayer for guidance.

"Would you prefer cookie sprinkles or candy-bar crumbles on your frozen yogurt?"

A slow smile spread across his face at the sound of Tara's voice. The curious mixture of Southern drawl and New York insistence had become his favorite interruption. He lifted his eyelids to see her hands outstretched, offering two cups of yogurt with sweet toppings.

The streetlamps backlit her hair casting a radiant auburn halo around the woman he loved. He loved the pale face and deep blue eyes, the hair that was her glorious crown, the sultry voice that haunted his dreams and the confident woman who had evolved from the lonely little girl.

He was in love with Tara Elliott. He'd fumbled his way to this moment in time and he was helpless to change things. She would never forgive him when the lies were exposed.

"Well?" She waved both desserts under his nose. "I'm good either way but make up your mind before the yogurt melts."

He accepted a vintage soda-shop cup and she took the loveseat beside his chair.

"Been out here long?" she queried with a casual air as she spooned cookies and cream into her mouth.

"A few minutes." He grasped the spoon and dug in to his dessert.

"You should have joined us." Tara appeared nonchalant, watching the foot traffic on the campus across the street.

"I did." His spoon clinked on the cup as he enjoyed the treat and the way she fished for details.

"So, you were listening," she stated.

"And thinking," he added.

"Listening and thinking. That's good." Her head bobbed up and down. "That's very good."

"Could I get one of those workbooks you were talking about?" He might as well give her what she wanted or she'd never be satisfied.

"A Gospel-study workbook?" Her beautiful eyes widened. "Sure, and I have an extra study Bible I can loan to you if you need one."

He dropped all casual pretence and set his cup on the flat chair arm. He leaned forward and laid his hand on her knee, covered as usual by black cotton trousers. "Thank you for inviting me. I'm sorry I didn't come inside, but I heard enough from out here to want to hear more. I'd appreciate the workbook and the Bible. I have a lot of work to do and I hope you'll be patient with me."

She pressed a warm palm atop his fingers and squeezed. "I'm not the one you have to ask for patience, Sam. I felt called to make the Word and the group available to you and now that I've done my part, where you go from here is between you and God."

"And where I have dinner Saturday night is between you and me." He changed the subject.

"Is that so?" Her blue eyes flashed.

"Yes it is." He made a show of unfolding the auction certificate he pulled from his hip pocket. "According to this, I am entitled to a private tour of Sycamore House Saturday evening to be followed by a gourmet dinner in the formal dining room, to be prepared, served and shared by the homeowner."

"Let me see that." She snatched the paper from his grip. "This doesn't say all that. It's a receipt for your charitable contribution."

He wrapped his fingers around her wrist and pulled the paper closer. "No, check it out. Read the fine print."

She leaned in to get a better view. "What fine print?"

As their faces came together over the page, his senses filled with her spicy scent. "Hmm," he murmured. "My mistake."

As the evening shadows fell across the porch in front of Bridges, Sam wanted desperately to kiss her. But he had too much to think about to confuse his senses further. Sam exhaled an unsteady breath. "Now, about that dinner." He pretended to be calm.

His near loss of composure was music to her ears. She pushed to her feet and retrieved the abandoned dessert cups.

"Okay, if you insist." She feigned resignation. "Saturday night, seven o'clock." Before she crossed the threshold into the store, she cast him a wink and a sly smile. "Bring the extra helmet."

Chapter Fifteen

Right on time, a familiar rumble crescendoed up
the long drive on Sycamore. Tara scrubbed her teeth,
plopped her toothbrush into the plastic cup, dabbed
her mouth and practiced a demure smile. She flut-
tered her eyelashes, moistened her lips with the tip
of her tongue and heaved a sigh at her ridiculous behavior.

"What is wrong with me?" she pleaded with the
mirror above the sink. The deep blue eyes that stared
back from the pale face gave her a "get real" glare.
"Okay, so I can answer my own question. But what
good is knowing I'm still in love with Sam when a
commitment is the last thing he's interested in?"

She stepped back to admire the new sundress
Lacey had sent over. The silky blue matched her eyes
and it fit perfectly, ending in a soft swirl around her
knees.

The doorbell chimed. Too self-conscious for a last peek, she ran a brush through loose curls without glancing at the mirror, stepped into new sandals and padded down the stairs. She stood before the door with a hand over her heart to slow the hammering. "It's only a casual evening," she whispered as she smoothed her hands over the front of the new dress. "Yeah, right."

She swept the heavy wooden door aside as Sam reached for the screen with his left hand. He let out a long, low wolf whistle as he presented her with a bouquet of familiar summer flowers, haphazardly bunched in his right fist.

"Oh, Sam, they're lovely." She took the offering and stepped aside, ducking her head so he wouldn't see her pleasure at his very male reaction to her sundress.

"Then you're not mad at me for picking them?"

"You picked these out of *my* flower bed?" She turned and smacked her open palm against his solid bicep.

"Well—" he ducked a second swing "—nobody was enjoying them out there and I thought they'd be nice on your table." He accompanied her into the kitchen where a mischievous smile spread across his face. "Great minds think alike," he teased. A mound of clippings littered the tiled counter around a tall crystal vase holding a rainbow assortment of backyard blossoms.

"What *is* that smell?" His attention shifted as he sniffed, closing his eyes to savor the aroma.

"Eventually it will be beef Wellington in puffed pastry with steamed vegetables and hollandaise sauce. We have chocolate crème brûlée for dessert," she proudly announced.

"Delicious." He sniffed the air and moved nearer.

Goose bumps skittered across her bare shoulders. She shivered and backed away. "Oh, no you don't. We have an agenda for the evening and you're not going to distract me and make me burn this expensive dinner that I've worked on all day."

"Yeah, I can see that." He surveyed the kitchen, where she'd obviously been experimenting with one disastrous recipe after another.

"Well, I want you to get your money's worth."

"Will you stop worrying about the money?" He turned, leaned his palms against the edge of the porcelain sink and surveyed the backyard through one of the tall kitchen windows.

"When did Miss Miriam put in the greenhouse?"

She stood beside him. "Almost five years ago. The woodwork already needs paint."

"Let's go take a look."

"You're not here to investigate my maintenance needs."

"No, but I am here for a tour of the house and I'd like to start out back."

Recognizing the tone that said his mind was

made up, she reached into the freezer and drew out two frosted mugs. "If you insist, let's take our drinks and sit in the gazebo." Ice cubes clinked into the glasses and sweet tea gurgled to the rims. She plopped a sprig of mint on each and handed one to Sam. He gulped half his drink in a single swallow and rattled his ice for a refill.

"I presume that means you approve." She smiled and poured.

"Of everything."

She accepted the compliment with a nod and led the way through the kitchen door to the yard they both knew so well. They followed the brick pathway and stepped into the muggy confines of the greenhouse that had once sheltered a small but honorable collection of rare flowers.

"What was on these shelves?" Sam could see the automatic misters and spotlights set up for display.

"Grandmother's prizewinning orchids. I donated them to the horticulture department."

"That was generous of you."

She waved away his compliment. "It was either that or let them die from lack of attention. I have no patience or skill with growing things. Even the silk plants in my apartment are neglected and dusty."

"Are you going to give up your place in New York?" he questioned. He seemed to study the systems installed to control the temperature and humidity of the nursery.

"Not right away." She watched for his reaction to her plans. "I still haven't made the decision to leave The Heritage. If I stay on, I can afford to hire someone to manage Bridges and that'll create another job for somebody who might get laid off from the college."

"What about Sycamore House?" He turned his smoky gaze to her. His scrutiny combined with the humidity in the greenhouse was suddenly unbearable. She pressed the icy glass to her cheek, stepped through the door and headed for the shady gazebo with Sam close behind.

"I should be able to make frequent visits."

"But this place needs a constant caregiver. You're right about the trim needing a new coat." He flicked at curling chips of paint on the latticework as they ducked into the shade and sank into comfortable cushions on wicker chairs. "I noticed the garden needs to be weeded and you'll have to put in a lot of new plants in the fall."

Tara hadn't been aware of much concerning the house in the few months she'd been there. It was her home but with her constant flurry of work and fundraising it had been little more than a place to shower and sleep. Sam was right. An old place needed constant care or it would fall apart before your eyes.

"I haven't had time to think this through." She chewed her lip. "I'm not sure I could afford a live-in caretaker."

"You could always bulldoze this place and put up something modern and low-maintenance instead."

The tea in Tara's glass sloshed as she turned to see if Sam was teasing her. His eyes were serious, narrowed as he surveyed the large backyard.

"You have over three acres that could easily accommodate a pool and tennis court as long as you're updating the property."

"I have no intention of bulldozing anything. I love this place. It's my home."

His eyes darkened. "Then why did you abandon it?"

Tara's face had been flushed from the moment she'd opened the door and given him a gander at the new dress. Where her usual black garb served to deflect attention, this wisp of blue fabric begged to be appreciated.

The hothouse had intensified the blush he found so endearing and now his suggestion that she level the historic property had her cheeks in full bloom. Little did she know his heart hammered at the mention of her return to New York and he suspected he had some telltale color of his own beneath his dark tan.

He'd intended to keep the evening lighthearted but even the *possibility* of Tara returning to her life in New York had delivered a punch to his gut. It brought home the reality of the situation as nothing else did. Sooner or later she'd find out about his holdings and when she did, she'd leave. It was only a matter of time before he lost the woman he loved.

Tara hung her head. She picked at the white wicker as she appeared to consider his question. He saw her chest rise and fall while she took in deep breaths. Her eyes closed for a few moments and he suspected she was praying.

Her head tilted up and the full force of her ocean-blue eyes washed over him. "The truth is I left because I was ashamed and angry over what happened to you."

He held his palms outward to stop her but she continued.

"No, Sam, you need to let me say this."

Her fingers pressed insistently atop his knee. He felt the warmth of her touch through his faded jeans. It burned into him even when she jerked her hand away as if she felt it too.

"As you've reminded me many times, you remember everything I said that day in your classroom." She made no effort to slow the color that crept up her throat. "I wasn't playing schoolgirl games with you, Sam. I'd been praying and studying on the subject of a Godly mate and since you were active in church back then, every road led me straight to you. Some of the most meaningful moments in my life up till that point had involved you.

"There were so many times when kids wouldn't

include me in their games, but I could always count on Thursdays with you. When I hated standing out like Bozo the Clown, you called me Rusty and said my hair made me special. You won my heart, Sam." She blinked back the tears that threatened. "I can't remember my mother's face, but everything about those days with you is etched into my memory." Her voice broke.

She paused for a sip of her tea and he noticed how the ice in her glass clinked from the shaking of her hand. He didn't deserve, and he couldn't bear to witness her raw emotions.

"I know this is important," he interrupted. "And we can continue this conversation later if you still want to say these things. But could we stop here and go for a ride before it gets dark? There's something I'd like to show you." He held out his hand.

She heaved what sounded like a sigh of relief, gave him a small smile and slipped her palm into his.

Ten minutes later when she reappeared in sneakers and jeans, her hair pulled into a tight braid, he almost regretted his offer to take her for a ride.

"Promise me you'll put that dress on and let your hair down when we get back?"

"If you insist." She rolled her eyes. Her composure had returned.

"Oh, I insist."

The sky still glowed from the persistent rays of

a sweltering summer sun. Longer days meant late-evening sunset cruises. At the outskirts of Beardsly, the bike roared to life and ate up the hot pavement.

Several minutes into the ride, Tara relaxed her hold on his waist. He rejected the obvious ploy of swerving to miss a pothole so she'd tighten her grip. Instead, he resorted to dipping low on a wide curve. It was a cheap trick, but it worked. Tara hugged him close, her heartbeat pressed to his spine, and he was at peace for the first time in months.

With no traffic in sight, he pulled the bike to the shoulder of the road. The Lake o' the Pines Bridge stretched before them. Sam cut the engine and dropped the kickstand. Following his lead, she removed her helmet.

"See that stretch of cleared shoreline right there?" He slid off the bike, wrapped an arm around her shoulders and angled her so she could site down the length of his arm.

"The place where the pegs stick up out of the water?"

"That's it. Those are pilings for the dock. There's three hundred feet of shoreline extending from that yellow flag over there to just below the bridge, down that way." He indicated the boundaries with pride. "It's five acres of wooded property. Hardwoods, too, not scruff pine. According to the agent, it's been on the market less than a week."

"It's beautiful. I'm sure some technology mogul

from California will snap it up, mow down the trees, put his summer house too close to the water and sue the county because the bridge blocks the view."

"I don't think so," he disagreed. "Not on that spot, anyway."

She leaned back and squinted as if getting a closer look at him. "What are you up to?"

"Nothin'," he insisted. "I have a hunch somebody who cares about this land will do right by it."

She glanced in the direction he'd pointed and then back at him, her eyes wide with suspicion. "You're not thinking of getting some of your *friends* to invest in that property, are you, Sam?"

"And if I am?" He baited her.

"Then they'll be right up the road from us and you'll become an accessory to whatever they're up to out here." A sharp shake of her head pulled curls free from the braid. He tugged a thin strand of the auburn silk and caressed it between his thumb and index finger.

"You worry too much, Rusty."

"And you don't seem to worry at all, which worries me even more."

Unable to resist any longer, he grasped both her elbows and tugged her against his chest. She gave a small gasp of surprise as he slanted his mouth across hers.

* * *

Sam raised his head but continued to hold her to his chest. She felt his heart thumping double-time compared to her own. He drew a breath to speak but hesitated.

"What?" she encouraged.

He kissed the top of her head as he held her in the tender embrace. She felt his warm breath as a sigh escaped. "What is it, Sam?" she asked again.

"Just don't worry about me, Rusty. I know you feel guilty for what happened, but my life hasn't turned out so bad."

She closed her eyes and said a short prayer for the strength to walk away with her head held high when the time came. She gave him a hard squeeze and as she pushed away she teased, "You're going to be the one who feels guilty if my dinner is dried out when we get home."

"Then home it is." He bowed and extended his arm toward the bike with a flourish. "M'lady, your trusty steed awaits."

Mouthwatering aromas radiated from the kitchen at Sycamore House. Sam pitched in to get the meal on the table, filling the water goblets and placing fat pats of butter and flaky rolls on each bread plate. Flickering candles flanked the riot of colorful blooms that formed the table's centerpiece.

"Dinner is served," she announced with pride as

she approached the dining-room table carrying a platter laden with beef Wellington.

Over steamed carrots, fresh green beans and mushrooms with pearl onions, they feasted on the juicy tenderloin and laughed about what seemed like very old times. Memories became a game of trivia as they recalled moments the two of them had experienced together.

"I'll never forget that bug collection." She rolled her eyes and shivered.

"You didn't do anything but squeal and hold the jar," he reminded her. "I did all the dirty work."

"And God bless you for that, Sam. I'd still be in sixth-grade science if you hadn't taken pity on me."

"I owed you one for getting me through freshman civics."

"Michigan?" She quizzed him without warning.

"Lansing," he fired back.

"Rhode Island?" she demanded.

"Providence," he said with a smug smile.

"Wisconsin?"

"Madison."

"See? I told you once you got them down you'd never forget."

"You may have given me too much credit." He laughed and shook his head. "Years ago I was on a ten-day ride with a dozen other bikers from Houston to Maryland and back. When we stopped in Atlanta, I made a comment to our waitress about the gold-domed building downtown and asked if it was a museum. When she told me it was the capitol building, I hung my head like a fool. The guys wouldn't let me lead the ride for the rest of the day."

She smiled at the story. "Sam, if I've ever known a man who didn't deserve to call himself a fool, it's you."

His eyes twinkled with interest. "What makes you say that? I've made some pretty foolish choices over the years."

"If you have, you seem to have learned from them and nothing's holding you back from success now."

She reached for his empty dinner plate and stood to clear the table. He jumped to his feet and reached for the serving platter.

"Sit down." She swatted his hand away. "You're a paying guest, not the busboy."

"I want to help," he insisted.

"Then come start the coffee while I glaze our crème brûlée. Would you like to have dessert in the library?"

His eyes revealed his appreciation of her suggestion. As a boy, he'd often expressed his fascination for the room filled floor to ceiling with hundreds of volumes. His love for knowledge was a perfect fit for the room and the room was the perfect setting for the confessions she was determined to make.

* * *

Tara used a mini blowtorch to crystallize the sugar atop their custard while Sam attended to the coffeemaker. As they hummed along with the radio, a shiver of déjà vu shot up his spine. How many times, as kids, had they experienced the same companionable quiet in this kitchen? Categorizing bugs, memorizing multiplication tables and gluing planets onto their solar system orbits.

From the very beginning, they'd been comfortable together, understanding one another's needs and fears without words. No wonder he'd been her primary candidate when her thoughts had turned to marriage. All these years later, Tara appealed to him for those same reasons. And so many more.

But the things they had in common were no match for the deceptions he'd committed. No shame she felt the need to confess could compare with the guilt he'd bear the rest of his life once his lies were exposed.

He'd begun to pray again. Selfish prayers for a way out of the web that held him fast. God had already spoken to Sam's heart and he knew what had to be done. Tonight was the night.

"That was delicious," he complimented the sweet, creamy custard.

"You think so?" she asked, reluctant to accept his praise.

"The entire meal was excellent, don't you reckon?" He leaned forward to set his cup and saucer on the centuries-old sea chest that served as a coffee table in the private library. "Worth every penny of my donation." He winked and held up a hand to stop her protest over the money. "Thank you for going to so much trouble."

She twisted on the sofa to face him and modestly tugged the silky dress over her bare knees. "I need to finish what I started in the garden earlier and I hope it won't spoil your dinner."

With his heart aching from the worried frown on her face, he smiled to put her at ease and took her hand gently in his. "Don't worry. Just say what's on your mind."

She squeezed his fingers and stared with huge blue eyes. "What happened almost ten years ago was all my fault, Sam. You were like a big brother to me for years and I had no right to imagine our friendship could ever be more than that. I was so ashamed when you left Beardsly. I knew if I'd just kept my fantasies to myself you would have stayed here, living out your dream and I'd at least have had you for my friend. But because I was determined to have my say, it cost you more than anyone could have imagined. I realize that no matter how hard I try, I can never make it up to you."

"There's no need to make anything up to me, Rusty. You were being true to yourself by following your heart. I understand that now, much more than you know."

"I hope you'll be able to forgive me for doing it again, but I can't help myself." Her gaze dropped to where their fingers were twined together. "I love you," she whispered.

He couldn't have heard correctly. His heart ricocheted against his rib cage. The noise thundered in his ears, drowning out all sound. He ducked his head to make eye contact with Tara. Their eyes met and the message in her electric gaze sent a shock through his system.

"I love you, Sam," she repeated. "I never stopped loving you. Not ever."

He was light-headed with hope and fear at the same time. "I don't know what to say," he muttered stupidly.

"Don't say anything yet, because that's not all." She took a deep breath and hurried on. "Grandmother had this cockamamy idea that if we were thrown together again, we'd find true love and live happily ever after. I knew that was her intention the day the will was read."

She looked down to where she squeezed his hand tightly, as if for the last time. "Instead of telling you this months ago, I went along with it, hoping she might be right, praying Grandmother's scheme would work. But I'm finally accepting the fact that anything built on a false foundation is doomed to fail."

Tara lifted glistening eyes. "At the risk of having you reject me again, Sam, I had to tell you the truth." She exhaled with a loud whoosh and gave him a lopsided smile as a tear trickled down her cheek.

He untangled his fingers from hers and lifted his hand to trace a gentle touch over the wet streak. He couldn't force words past the lump in his throat, stuck there since the moment of her timid "I love you."

A faraway sound penetrated the bubble of emotion that encased the cozy study. The high-pitched whine became an annoying alarm as it grew closer. Finally a shrill siren pierced the air demanding attention. Flashes of red light flickered across the walls as the wailing engine streaked past Sycamore House.

Tara gasped when the phone jangled on the sofa table behind them. Sam turned and grabbed the receiver, placing it in her hand. All trace of color fled from her face and her eyes flew wide in horror as she dropped the phone and jumped to her feet.

"It's the Elliott Building!"

Chapter Sixteen

In the wee hours of the morning, the final smoldering heat was no match for the scalding tears that burned Tara's eyes. Sam had left her side moments earlier to accompany the volunteer fire chief in an effort to survey what was left of the gutted brick structure.

As they'd watched in horror, the floor of Bridges had crumbled with a ghastly groan, sending the charred contents of her store plummeting atop the remains of Sam's shop. There was no need to wait for the official report. Beneath the streetlamps of the town square it was evident to everyone that the building was a total loss.

"Let's get you home," Lacey insisted. She stood with her arm wrapped around her friend, the position Sam had left minutes before. "There's nothing you can do here tonight and tomorrow you'll need a clear head when you talk to your insurance agent."

"That will be a very brief conversation." Tara's heart, giddy with relief a few hours earlier, was once again heavy with guilt. And this time it was all hers to bear, all her fault, all of her own making. No grandmother had pulled the strings. No Board of Regents had rushed to interfere. The blame was hers and hers alone.

"What do you mean?" Lacey questioned.

"I never increased the insurance," Tara admitted. "The building is covered under the old policy, but the contents are lost." Hours ago, like a storm surge, the realization had hit as Sam stood with his arm around her, a shield of protection. If not for his strength and support, she'd have crumpled to the ground under the weight of the moment as sure as the landmark structure across the street was crumbling before their eyes.

"But you had the papers. I saw them myself on your desk in Bridges."

"And Sam made a special trip to the house to remind me to notarize and file them. I know exactly where they are. Where they…*were*," she corrected as she stared through gritty eyes at the remains of their joint inheritance.

Sam's shop. His last hope.

"He'll understand, Rusty. Together you'll find a way to work this out."

"I can't tell him."

"If you don't, the insurance company will. The chief said they'll be out from Dallas as soon as the investigator's final report is filed. Four days at the most."

"That should be enough." Tara mentally calculated the time she'd need for the dreaded task. As much as she hated even considering what she had to do, it was the only way to make things right.

"Enough for what?" Lacey stepped in front of Tara, placing a hand on either shoulder. "Tell me what you're planning."

"I'm going to use the one asset I have left. Grandmother's collection is worth a small fortune. At auction they'd bring considerably more, but I don't have that kind of time. I'm going to offer them directly to that dealer in Houston who's been pestering me. I know he'll snap everything up and then I'll have the money to replace Sam's stock and get Bridges going again."

"Listen to me." Lacey gave Tara a brief shake. "Tell Sam everything. Together you may be able to find another way."

"I can't," Tara insisted. "It's taken me ten years to put things right between us. His bitterness has turned to contentment these past couple of months and he's come back to God. If he finds he's lost everything again, thanks to me, he may not get over it this time. I'm the one left with a house full of valuable antiques and he's left with nothing, so we're right back where we started."

"I don't agree, but I see what you mean."

"Sam's such an honest businessman, so full of personal integrity, he'd expect me to take responsibility for what I've done and handle matters myself. I pray to God that'll make it easier for him to forgive me…again."

"This fire is not your fault. Anything could have caused it."

Tara shook her head, recalling orange flames and black plumes of smoke escaping from the upstairs windows as they arrived on the scene. "I can't remember checking the espresso machine when I left. That could be it." She turned her head toward the charred ruins.

"No matter how it started, it's still not your fault and the sooner you get that through your head the better. Don't waste energy on self-recrimination. It's going to take everything you have for the next few months to rebuild and start over."

"I don't have a few more months." Tara closed her eyes and massaged her temples as one more realization surfaced. "I have to be back in New York in a week."

"Maybe Ethan will extend your leave."

"That's not an option. He made it perfectly clear before he left. Time's up. They need me back at work or they're going to fill my position."

Lacey pulled Tara into a comforting hug. "*Father, we know all things work together for the good of those who love You,"* Lacey began. *"We ask You to use this painful time to strengthen the bond between Tara and Sam and to teach them a new and powerful truth that will bless them forever. Amen."*

"Thank you," Tara whispered past the knot in her throat.

Heavy footsteps came to a stop at her side and a large, warm hand rested on the small of her back. She raised her head to stare into the steely depths of Sam's eyes.

"There's nothing we can do tonight," he confirmed. "Let's go home and get some rest so we can start fresh in the morning. We have a lot to do."

"Sam, I'm so sorry." Her voice broke.

He opened his arms and she stepped from Lacey's hug and found herself folded in Sam's strong embrace.

"Don't apologize, Rusty. Accidents happen. It'll take some time but we'll rebuild. That's what insurance is for."

The congregation spilled through the front doors of the church, squinting against the bright sunlight. Conversation was split between the pastor's message, the previous weekend's fund-raiser and the fire at the Elliott Building. The common thread was the grace of God and the many forms it takes.

The final tally for Texas Treasure Days had exceeded everyone's expectations. Dean Grant was making the rounds of all the worship services, showing his appreciation to the citizens of Beardsly for their generosity and support.

Pastor Ryan gave heartfelt thanks that it was property and not lives lost in last night's fire. He reminded his flock, "Only treasures stored up in heaven will last. For where your treasure is, there your heart will be also."

Tara sat beside Sam, her eyes downcast during most of the service, her mind a whirlwind of mixed emotions. The pleasure of his arrival to accompany her to worship was clouded by the turmoil over her secret plans to sell her grandmother's possessions. The drama of the fire had so overshadowed her words of love that she'd begun to wonder if Sam even remembered them.

Out in the parking lot, friends expressed their support. As Sam stood tall and accepted handshakes, he insisted over and over that the loss of his business was just another of life's learning experiences. Tara noted his relaxed stance and confident smile. Even after the night's ordeal and their terrible financial setback he was calm and at ease.

Her stomach churned at the thought of destroying what little peace he'd found. The importance of her mission grew with each passing moment. There was one chance to make it right and she prayed fervently that she was doing God's will.

* * *

"You gonna be all right?" Sam asked as they walked the pathway from the garage to the front porch.

"After I take a nap and think all this through, I guess I will be." She twisted the knob that was never locked and the screen door creaked open. "Would you like to come in?"

He'd like nothing better, but until this crisis was past, he couldn't risk time alone with Tara. Her declaration of love had almost been his undoing. He'd been about to fall to his knees and confess his own feelings when the call came from the fire station.

God was giving Sam a chance to fix things. If he rode to her rescue like a white knight, maybe he'd be forgiven for all his deceptions. He could keep a calm head, manage all the work to be done, make the building even better than before and see to it that Tara had everything she needed to get started again.

Somehow, he'd break the news to the town that he had significant resources of his own and wanted to share them with his lady love and his community. Everyone would forgive him. He was betting his heart on it.

"Thanks for asking, but I can see you need some rest. I have a lot of business calls to make and I'm heading back to Houston this afternoon to set the wheels in motion to replace my stock."

"So soon?" He heard the panic in her voice. "I mean, don't we need to worry about the building first?"

"Once the investigation is complete and the insurance company releases the funds, you're going to be amazed at how soon I get that building restored." He ran his hand down the back of her silky braid and pulled her to his chest.

"We'll need to be prepared to move back in right away."

She tucked her head and sniffed back a rush of tears.

"I'm sorry, Rusty," he soothed. "I've been all wrapped up in my own plans and you have a much tougher job ahead of you replacing the pieces you had in Bridges."

He put his thumb beneath her chin and tipped her head back. "Tell you what. Give me a week to settle things and I'm yours for as long as you need my help." He meant it from the core of his soul. If she'd have him, he intended to be hers and hers alone for the rest of their lives.

He placed a light kiss on the tip of her nose. "Deal?"

"Deal." Her eyes were huge in her pale face. "Listen, I'm going to follow your example and get to work contacting some antique dealers. So, I might take a day trip myself tomorrow."

"That's a great idea," he encouraged. "Sitting

around here won't accomplish much right now, so get busy and stay focused on the future."

He dropped his arms to his sides reluctantly and backed away. "I'll check in with you in a couple of days."

The screen door banged behind her as she let herself into the house. Even draped in black again, her figure took his breath away. She was a beautiful woman in every way possible.

"Rusty?"

She turned and stared wide-eyed at him.

"I remember what you said last night." He admired the endearing blush that crept into her cheeks. "Can you give me a little time to think about everything?"

"I've waited ten years. What can a few more days possibly hurt?"

On Monday morning Sycamore House was a mess and Tara was exhausted, but she felt armed and dangerous for the day's mission. She climbed into the land yacht at daylight and headed for Houston. On the leather seat beside her a cardboard box was filled with facts on the Miriam Elliott collection.

Tara had spent Sunday afternoon updating her records with digital photographs to accompany the official provenance of each piece of furniture and artwork. Armoires were pulled away from walls, tabletops were cleared, display cabinets were emptied and upholstered chairs were turned upside down to reveal intricately carved legs.

She prayed the collector who'd called three times since her grandmother's death would offer top dollar, but she was prepared to settle for less if it meant a sale. Today.

As the skyline of Houston loomed in the distance, she prepared her heart for the job ahead.

"Heavenly Father," she spoke out loud. *"I don't believe You brought me to this moment to let me fail. There is a reason why Sam is back in my life after all these years. I know Grandmother orchestrated things, but it is You who ordains them. As much as I want to be with Sam, I want Your will to be done in my life even more. Please give me the strength to handle whatever this day holds. Amen."*

She fed the sedan into the morning traffic that crawled through the sprawling city and followed the directions to the Westheimer Antique Gallery.

Over breakfast, lunch and afternoon tea she bonded with the gallery owner and wrangled the best possible price for her heirlooms. The gallery's fleet of trucks would arrive at Sycamore House by nine the following morning to take possession of the sale items. With a lump in her throat the size of the Astrodome, Tara climbed into her car and set the tiny black clutch that held the huge cashier's check close to her side.

She sniffed into the handkerchief the owner had insisted she accept as she signed the papers. Still clutching the linen square, she eased the car onto the new toll road, dabbing at bittersweet tears that slid from her eyes.

She allowed herself a deep breath and loud exhale. "Okay, that's it. No more crying. I should be celebrating." She patted the purse beside her. "And as soon as I get north of the city and this dreadful stretch of traffic, I'm going to indulge in a cola. And not one of those diet things, either. Today I've earned caffeine *and* sugar."

The radio blared lively country music as she took the interstate that would lead her east for four hours to Beardsly. Close to the city limits the traffic began to thin and she spotted a fast-food emblem on the upcoming exit sign. Her mouth watered at the thought of a double cheeseburger to go with that drink.

Pulling into the exit lane, she squinted to study billboards rising above the pine trees a hundred yards ahead. Too far away to make out more than a word or two, the massive signs advertised everything from motels to music stores. On the tallest tower of all the word *motorcycles* caught her attention.

As cars inched closer to the intersection, she continued to glance toward the familiar orange trademark on the sign. As the full force of the billboard's message struck home, she stomped the brake. The pickup truck on her rear bumper screeched to a halt as the driver blew the horn and gave her an ugly gesture.

Tara was barely aware of the commotion she was causing on the crowded feeder street. Her heart pounded in her chest and she gasped for air, open-mouthed and wide-eyed as a guppy. The sign ahead read Sam Kennesaw Cycles.

"Sam, you need to step out here immediately." Claire's always cultured voice carried over the intercom with a hint of panic. "Tara Elliott has just walked into the showroom."

He pushed to his feet so fast his Windsor chair rolled backward and banged against the wall behind his desk.

"What did you say?" He stared at the speakerphone, certain he'd misunderstood.

"Excuse me, Miss. You can't go back there. That's Mr. Kennesaw's private office," Claire called from the end of the hall.

Heels clicked on the terra-cotta-tile floor as the intruder approached his open door. Sam stepped around his desk. His heart pounded. His ribs ached. Fine perspiration broke out across his forehead.

"Mr. Kennesaw and I are old friends." Tara stood in the doorway. "He doesn't keep any secrets from me." She nailed him with her piercing blue eyes. "Do you, Sam?"

"Sam, I'm sorry," Claire apologized. She looked over Tara's shoulder, her blond eyebrows drawn together, her pretty face a mask of sympathy.

"It's okay, Claire. The lady's right. We are old friends and she's welcome in my office." He waved Claire away.

"Is that so?" Tara quizzed. She stepped into his professional sanctuary and ran her hand along the edge of his valuable turn-of-the-century partners' desk. "I'm welcome in your office, but I'm still not welcome in your life."

"That's not true, Rusty."

"Don't call me that," she snapped. "The boy who gave me that name was my dearest friend. He was my heart. He was my love."

"He still is." Sam inched toward her, as if any sudden move would crack her composure. But he noted, for once, her skin was clear and fair in an emotional moment. She was in complete control, which scared him even more.

"It's all been a game for you, hasn't it, Sam? You saw your opportunity for payback and you couldn't resist."

"I admit that *was* true." He held both palms outward in his defense. "But only at first. You have to believe me," he pleaded.

"Believe you?" She snorted and rolled her eyes

toward the ceiling before impaling him with a chal-
lenging stare. "Believe the down-and-out guy who
accepted my grandmother's generosity so he could
have a last chance to make something of himself?"

She glanced at his silk wall hangings. "Believe
the dirt-poor fella who lives in cheap student hous-
ing because he can't afford anything better?"

She took several slow steps toward him. "Believe
the struggling business owner who has to have questionable financing to survive? Or the pied piper who
tells all the kids it's not how much you have, but
how much you give that matters?

"Which one of those men would you have me believe, Sam?" She punctuated her question by slap-
ping her black purse on his desktop so hard the clasp
broke, scattering the contents on the carpeted floor.

A shiver of defeat ran through his body. There
was no defense for what he'd done. His determination to settle the score had turned an omission of the
truth into a lie that controlled every aspect of his
duplicitous life. And the crazy part was that the life
he'd concocted in Beardsly was far more appealing
and fulfilling than his real existence.

"Will you hear me out, please?" He gestured toward the plush sofa, but she ignored him and stood
her ground. "I've already admitted it," he began.
"You're right. It was all about a pound of flesh. I
wanted you to have a small taste of the loss I suffered because of you."

"You don't seem to have suffered too much." She swept her hand to indicate the wealthy trappings of his office.

"In the big picture, no, I haven't. In fact, I've recently realized that being forced out of Beardsly was the best thing that ever happened to me. Being forced to make it on my own made coming home that much sweeter." Pulse racing, he risked a step closer, hoping for a break in her rock-solid calm. "And living a lie all these weeks made falling in love with you that much more frightening."

Her expression never changed. He watched as she stooped to gather up the things strewn from her purse. She reached toward the small wallet and papers and her hand froze above the familiar Persian rug. The tree-of-life pattern was identical to the carpet in her home that she'd always believed was one of a kind. As the realization that he'd led her on about that subject dawned, she probably reasoned that every conversation he'd had with her for months had been a lie. She brushed her fingertips across the intricate weave. Then, clutching her possessions, she stood and crossed the remaining gap that separated them.

"How dare you mention love to me?" Her voice quivered when she spoke. "All I ever wanted was you. And now I see all you ever wanted was what belonged to me. Well, you've won, Sam."

She turned a slip of paper over in her hand and

thrust it into his face. He read the words *Westheimer Gallery* on the six-figure cashier's check.

"It's all yours now. What's left of the Elliott Building, Sycamore House and this, the money from the sale of Grandmother's antiques."

Unable to believe what he was hearing, he reached for the check, but she crammed everything back into her bag.

"Like a fool, I forgot to handle the insurance upgrade. The only way to make it up to you was to sell everything that was mine, just as grandmother's idea of making things up to you was to give you everything that was hers. Including me."

His guts churned with the force and reality of her words. He knew his next admission would twist the knife. "I don't need your money." He lowered his voice to soften the blow. "My shop was insured and I added enough coverage for the contents of the entire building as a precaution."

Her lips curved in a brittle smile of surrender. Her naturally bright eyes were dull with the shock of his betrayal.

"You thought of every detail, didn't you, Sam? You had all your bases covered. You bought the town's goodwill and respect with parties and donations and you still have enough left over to develop lakefront property. All the things you coveted are finally yours.

"Well, let me remind you of something you heard

yesterday. Treasures stored up in Heaven are the ones that last. I hope you'll be happy with all your hard-earned material possessions, Sam. My conscience is clear." She pulled the check from her wallet and tossed it on the Persian carpet. "And now my debt to you is paid in full. I don't intend to lay eyes on you ever again."

Tara pivoted on her heel, crossed the room and disappeared through the door. He stood rooted to the spot, letting her go. She had every right to her anger. He didn't dare to presume he could make this horrible situation right in one conversation. In a day or two she'd be calm and willing to listen to reason.

He hoped.

"Sam?" Claire's voice was little more than a whisper. "Forgive me for eavesdropping, but it was obvious there was about to be a scene and I wanted to be able to help if either of you needed it."

He sank into the chair behind his desk and dropped his head into his hands. "I've managed to foul things up so much that nobody can help me this time."

From her position beside his chair, she dropped to her knees and scooped his trembling hands into hers. "It sounds like you've been wrong a lot lately and you're wrong about this, too. You *can* make things right with Tara, but you need to make things right with God first."

Sam closed his eyes and squeezed her hands and opened his heart to God the Father as Claire Savage prayed.

Chapter Seventeen

Dust swirled at the end of the driveway as the last cargo truck pulled away. Tara pressed a clenched fist to her lips to hold back the tears and stumbled to the privacy of the gazebo. Her resolve collapsed along with her knees as she dropped onto the wicker love-seat. The sobs she'd held inside for months burst free at last.

She wrapped tense arms around her body and let the tears flow as she rocked herself gently. Searing pain seeped out with hot tears. It coursed down her face and splashed on her black skirt. She cried for the mother she couldn't remember and the grandmother she'd never forget. She cried for the loss of her family and the loss of her home. She cried for the man she'd always love and the grief she couldn't escape.

Finally the tears trickled to a stop and dried on

her cheeks. She leaned her head back and stared at the bright blue sky through the latticework overhead. The color of heaven seeped through the white slats, washing warm comfort across her cold soul.

"Father, You don't force us to love You and I shouldn't have tried to manipulate Sam into loving me. Please forgive me for interfering with Your will and thinking I could take matters into my own hands. Give me the strength to get through this day and the peace to accept my yesterdays. I willingly give You all my tomorrows. Amen."

Resigned to finishing the job, she pushed to her feet and made her way past the vacant greenhouse into the nearly empty home. Hours earlier the rooms had been filled with solid pieces of history. Now they were almost deserted. Only a few items remained that she couldn't bear to part with. The moving van would pull into the drive tomorrow and impersonal hands would wrap her remaining prized belongings and pack them off to a storage vault in Manhattan.

"Anybody home?" Lacey called through the screen door.

Tara straightened her spine, tilted her chin upward and went to greet her lifesaver.

"Not for much longer," she answered and pasted on a determined smile as Lacey stepped into the foyer. The two friends hugged tightly.

"You know there are other ways to handle this," Lacey mumbled against Tara's shoulder.

"But this is the way that works for me." They walked arm-in-arm through the forlorn rooms.

"I need to put this all behind me as soon as possible and move on with my life. Grandmother meant well, and I gave it my best shot, but we were both wrong. The price for being wrong is high, but in this case it seems fair."

"You're a generous woman to give your home away, my friend," Lacey sniffed.

"I'm a *broken* woman with nothing more to lose." Tara squeezed Lacey's arm. "Believe it or not, it's almost a relief."

Lacey checked her wristwatch. "We still need to stop by Mr. Latimer's office. We'd better get on the road if you're going to make your flight tonight."

"My bags are on the porch. Are you sure you don't mind keeping an eye on things around here tomorrow? Mr. Latimer offered to handle it, you know."

"I wouldn't trust any man to oversee the packing of Miss Miriam's china and crystal." She gave a playful wink. "It will be my honor."

Tara's heels tapped softly across the mesquite floors for the last time. Her gaze swept over the staircase, across the entry to the dining room and through the cozy library. She blessed the home to the safekeeping of its new owner, turned and pulled the heavy door shut with a very final thump.

Wade Latimer was nothing if not efficient. True

to his word, the legal documents were prepared and waiting for her signature. He didn't bother with trivial conversation. With a glisten of sympathy in the kind eyes behind his glasses, he watched her sign away the cashier's check along with her remaining possessions.

Lacey took the back road away from town claiming it was a shorter route to the interstate. Tara knew better. It was to spare her a final view of the campus and the blackened ruins of the Elliott Building.

At three o'clock on a hot August afternoon, Tara whispered goodbye to the image of Beardsly, Texas, in her side-view mirror as it shrank to the size of a pecan and disappeared in the dust.

"I thought I might see you today," Lacey said when she answered the door at Sycamore House late the next morning.

Sam crossed the threshold and felt the weight of his lower jaw as it sagged with disbelief. He hadn't dreamed Tara would move so fast. Not only were the rooms empty but carpets were rolled up and artwork was boxed for storage. Professional packers bustled through the rooms wrapping glassware in brown paper and stacking the contents of the bookcases into sturdy corrugated boxes.

"Stop what you're doing, right now!" He shouted to get everyone's attention.

"Sam," Lacey calmed him and signaled for the

busy activity to continue. "They've been at this since daylight. They have orders to work straight through till everything's packed and loaded. The house will be empty and ready for you to take possession by tomorrow."

"Consider the orders changed."

"You don't have the authority to make that decision," Lacey informed him.

"Then who does?" He ran shaking fingers through his thick mop. Things were not going according to plan, which shouldn't surprise him since nothing had gone his way this past week. The world was tilted against its axis, spinning wildly out of orbit.

"Mr. Latimer has Tara's power of attorney concerning the remainder of Miss Miriam's estate."

"Where's Rusty? We have to talk." The big sedan was parked in the drive. She must be upstairs. Without waiting for Lacey's reply he bounded up the carved staircase, his boots clomping with heavy echoes as he checked first one empty bedroom and then another.

His feet slowed as he stood in the door of her girlhood sanctuary. His mind flashed back to a long-forgotten day when he'd tiptoed up the back stairs to get a secret glimpse of the second floor. A four-poster bed, so tall it required a stepping stool, had dominated the room. Topped by a white lace canopy and piles of fluffy pillows, it was angled beside the back windows of the house where curtains billowed in the warm breeze.

The bed was gone, the windows stripped of their coverings. The closet door stood ajar. Still feeling like an intruder, Sam crept across the floor and pulled the door wide. Bare padded hangers swung on the wooden rod. Shelves had been cleared with no trace of Tara remaining.

He closed his eyes and drew in a deep, sorrowful breath. As oxygen filled his lungs, the lingering scent of cinnamon drifted into his senses. His chin dropped to his chest and he gave in to the sob that escaped past the anxiety lodged in his throat.

For two nights he'd suffered in silence. Folded into the comfortable leather recliner in his spacious den, he'd stared out the floor-to-ceiling windows at his lagoon-style backyard pool. As recessed lights waltzed beneath the faux lily pads, visions of wooing Tara had danced in his mind. Being forgiven over a candlelit dinner, having her accept his proposal, agreeing to allow him to restore the Elliott Building and update the property surrounding Sycamore House were the fantasies of his sleepless nights.

He'd never once imagined that she'd be gone, leaving nothing but a faint trace of her spicy essence clinging to the closet shelves. Inside the dark enclosure he steadied himself against the wall and kept his eyes pressed tightly closed. As the long-forgotten feel of warm tears trickled down his cheeks, he recalled Claire's prayer and spoke the words aloud as best he could remember.

"Father, I've been so wrong about so many things in my life. Even so, You've blessed me beyond all I dreamed of. You made a way for me when my own way was blocked. Please, make a way for me now. I love Rusty. I've always loved the girl she was and now I adore the woman she's become. Lord, if it's Your will for our lives make a way for us to be together again."

He dragged the tail of his T-shirt across his eyes, relieved that the work was now in God's hands and thumped back down the steps.

"When did she leave?" he asked.

Lacey looked up from her work of slipping silverware into fuzzy cases. "Last night. She starts work on Monday so she had to get back to open her apartment and unpack."

He checked the time and glanced around at the stacks of moving boxes. "If you let these guys keep working it's just going to take you that much longer to put everything back the way they found it."

"Sam, this is what Tara wants."

He shook his head. "No, it's not. This is what she's accepting because she thinks I can't give her what she wants. She's wrong, Lacey. And you're going to help me prove it to her."

"Forgive me for interrupting your meeting, sir." Sam sat across from Wade Latimer in the same chair where the charade had begun three months earlier.

"I was expecting you, Sam. After Tara's sudden decisions yesterday I figured you'd want to make a full disclosure."

Sam's shoulders slumped. "So, she told you?"

Latimer removed his glasses, folded them carefully and laid them on the desk parallel with his ink blotter.

"Actually, I knew all along. Miriam did, too."

Sam sat ramrod-straight and narrowed his eyes to focus his full attention on the lawyer. "Knew what?"

"About your dealership, your home, your investments, your business associates. We did a full background check on you over a year ago when Miriam decided to update her will."

"Then why did you let me come in here and lie and take advantage of the situation?" Sam struggled to control his temper.

"It was what Miriam wanted. She didn't care how it played out as long as it brought you and her granddaughter together in the end."

Sam stood and paced the room. "I don't understand. Why would she change her mind all these years later after she let Tara talk her into running me off?"

"That's not how it happened at all." Latimer steepled his fingers and peered over them at Sam. "Yes,

Tara confided her feelings for you to her grandmother, but it was *Miriam* who made the decision to pull the funding for your scholarship. Tara begged her not to do it, but since Miriam had paid the bills all along she felt it was her decision to make."

"What do you mean 'paid the bills?'" Sam asked.

"I mean, Miriam Elliott funded your scholarship."

"Miss Miriam *personally* paid for my education?" Sam stood rooted to the spot letting the fact sink in. "But I applied for those scholarships and went through the interview process with the Board of Regents. There was no mention of a private benefactor."

"Because she didn't want you to feel beholden to her. She knew you and your mother would never accept charity so Miriam offered it in a way you couldn't refuse."

Sam shoved a lock of hair off his forehead and rested his jaw on his hand while he pondered the incredible news. The girl he'd blamed for upsetting his plans was never at fault. In fact, she'd fought for him to the detriment of her relationship with her only family member.

And the old woman he was so certain owed him restitution had secretly funded the education that had ultimately made him a financial success. As Ward Carlton would say, Sam felt as low as a snake's belly in a wagon-wheel rut.

Sam squeezed his eyes shut and ran his palms over his face. "Why didn't you stop me?" he mumbled through his fingers.

"I couldn't. I gave my word that I would let things take a natural course. You'd either find each other on your own or you'd go your separate ways. Miriam orchestrated the reason to get you young people together, but she left working out the details to God."

"As much as I'd like to be patient and wait to see what God has in mind now, I've got to do something. I love Tara, Mr. Latimer. This is her home and we have to find a way to bring her back." Sam's heart clutched with fear. Time was running out. "Will you help me?"

The older man smiled and rubbed his palms together. "What have you got in mind?"

"Hand me the phone directory." Sam pointed to the fat yellow book behind Latimer's desk. "While I call some heavy equipment operators, you get on the horn to that moving company at Sycamore House and order them to throw it into reverse."

The caller ID display on the portable handset read *Lacey Rogers*. Tara steadied herself with one hand on the dinette table in her New York apartment and punched the talk button.

"Lacey?" Tara knew in her gut this was bad news. "Tell me what happened."

"Oh, I wanted you to hear it from me. I guess one of your grandmother's nosy neighbors already called you."

Tara dropped into a chair, exhausted from the week's emotion and not certain she could take any more grief.

"Called me about what?"

"Honey, bulldozers went to work on the Elliott Building today. There won't be anything left but an empty lot by the end of the week."

Tara relaxed against the back of the chair. "That's sad, I know, but there was too much damage to do it any other way. The building has to be torn down and completely rebuilt. Is that all?"

"No, it's not. There's also a flatbed of heavy equipment parked in front of Sycamore House." The sound of Lacey's sigh resonated across the phone line. "Sam intends to level the old place and build a modern house on the property."

Tara shot to her feet. "He can't do that. I filled out the forms to have it declared an historic landmark."

"What did you do with the forms?"

"They were in my desk drawer…" Tara hung her head while another wave of injustice crashed over her. "…with the insurance papers."

"I tried talking to him but he's made up his mind. I'm sorry. There's nothing anyone can do."

"Oh, yes there is!" Tara was already in the bathroom throwing her toothbrush into a travel kit. "I'll be on the first flight to Dallas." She pulled an overnight bag from the closet, tossed it onto the bed and began stuffing it full.

"My grandmother loved that place and it's my home. Beardsly wouldn't be the same without it. I don't care if you have to become a human shield till I get there, don't let them harm a shingle on that house!"

"Now you're talking, girl," Lacey shouted as Tara tossed the phone onto the bed, stepped back into her black flats and headed for the door.

In a ladies' room at the Dallas–Fort Worth airport, Tara splashed water on her sticky skin and rebraided her hair. Bloodshot eyes stared back from a face even more pale than usual. She considered dabbing concealer on the dark circles beneath her eyes but passed on vanity in the interest of time.

A night in LaGuardia had given her a new perspective on the homeless, but it got her on the first flight south. She tossed her cosmetics into the carryon and made a mad dash to catch the rental car shuttle. To stay awake on the two-hour drive to Beardsly, she alternated between singing off-key and praying aloud. As activity in the square was coming to life she pulled down Main Street.

Even Lacey's warning couldn't prepare Tara for the jolt of seeing the Elliott Building. The charred exterior walls had been pushed down and only a giant pile of rubble remained of the once-proud structure. Front-end loaders were already in motion filling and emptying their huge buckets into waiting dump trucks. A twisted piece of metal that had once been a shiny chrome handlebar was a brutal reminder of her urgent destination. She accelerated toward Sycamore.

Even from a distance she spotted the long, low trailer pulled to the curb. The bright yellow equipment with huge wheels was poised to back down the ramp. Lacey's little red compact was slanted behind the transport trailer like a soup can before a school bus.

Lacey slammed the door as she jumped from her car and raced to meet the rented sedan. "I'm so glad you're here," she panted. They were threatening to lift my car and move it out of the way with a forklift."

"Get back in and stay put. We're not out of the woods yet." Tara swung up the long drive stomping on the brakes at the edge of the carport. She jumped from the rental and jogged up the wooden porch steps.

The door handle rattled at her touch. It was locked tight with the dead bolt thrown from inside. She rang the bell with one hand and relentlessly pounded the brass knocker with the other. Her persistence paid off as heavy footsteps thumped across the wooden floor of the foyer. The bolt slid open and the door inched back enough for Sam to poke his head out.

"Good morning, Rusty," he drawled.

"No, so far it's not," she fumed at his lazy smile.

"Well, it's bound to get better now that you're home. Don't you reckon?"

"It will get better when I have your assurance that those bulldozers won't leave that trailer."

"I'm sorry, but they have a lot of work to do today. I'm paying by the hour and if Lacey doesn't move her car soon the boys and I are gonna have to offer her some help."

The screen door remained locked between them or she'd have rewarded his casual attitude with a sharp elbow in the gut.

"Sam, come out here so we can talk. *Now*."

"It's ninety degrees in the shade out there," he observed. "How about if you come inside?" He made a slight move as if to open the door and then paused. "Under two conditions."

She took a cautious step away from the door. "What conditions?"

His smile faded. His eyes softened from smoky teasing to the kindest of gray. "That you let me do most of the talking and that you find it in you to forgive me."

The heavy weight on her heart shifted. She experienced a moment of calm and knew in her soul things were about to be put right, once and for all. Relieved to have such a spirit of peace she gave a small nod of agreement.

Sam flipped the lock and held the door open. "You'll have to excuse the mess."

"Mess? Didn't the movers clean up after themselves?" She spoke as she crossed the threshold into the cool, still quiet of the home she'd given away.

Sam's strong arms caught and held her fast when her knees buckled. Through a cloud of disbelief and fresh tears her gaze caressed the rooms before her. Where they had been lonely and empty days earlier, they were now filled with a lifetime's collection of heirlooms.

The Miriam Elliott Collection.

Sam continued to steady her from behind as she stumbled like a sleepwalker from room to room. The kitchen counter was splashed with color from backyard flowers lying beside an empty vase.

The Queen Anne chair and footstool were back in their cozy corner with the sea trunk positioned before the overstuffed sofa in the library. The hand-carved German curio cabinet once again displayed Hummel figurines near the griffin table that was laid out with two place settings for breakfast.

"Why, Sam?" She whispered the simple plea as she turned in his arms.

He pulled her to his chest, tucked her beneath his chin and stroked down the length of her back. She pressed her ear to his heart and heard the thumping that matched hers perfectly.

"Because I love you, Rusty," he murmured into her hair. "I realized it weeks ago but I was too much of a coward to admit it. I was afraid you'd change your mind about me when you found out I was lying, so I was waiting for the right moment to tell you the truth."

He kissed the top her head and held her to him, as if she'd cut and run. "I thought the fire was my perfect opportunity. I could come to the rescue and make everything better than before. And then you'd still love me."

She twined her arms around his waist, anchoring herself to the man she adored. "I've always loved you, Sam. I tried to force that love too soon and God used my grandmother to put years between us so I'd wait on His perfect timing. Knowing what He wanted for my life didn't give me the right to make it happen on my own."

Sam relaxed his hold so she could look into his eyes, the very portals of his soul. He bit his lower lip as it quivered with emotion. "Let's make it happen together, Rusty. But this time with God's help." His eyes glistened. "Please share my life. Please say you'll marry me."

"Are you serious?" she questioned him, amazed by his tender words.

His lips twitched and his chest rumbled with a

nervous chuckle. "If I hadn't been serious do you think I'd have paid twice what you got from the Westheimer Gallery to buy everything back for my bride's wedding gift?"

"Wouldn't you rather keep these things in Houston? That *is* your home after all."

He kissed her forehead. "I'm selling the dealership to Claire, who happens to be my business manager. So, my home is wherever you are. If you want it to be here, it'll be here. If you want it to be New York, it'll be New York."

"Sam, you're making a lot of big decisions in a hurry."

"That's because I'm in a hurry to have you for my wife. But I don't want to rush you into anything besides marriage. I know you love your job at The Heritage. If you want to keep it, I can live with that. I'll wait right here for you in Beardsly. I have plenty to do updating this place, restoring the Elliott building and volunteering at the college this fall."

A shiver of pleasure ran through her body at the thought of Sam back in the classroom. "There's nowhere I'd rather be than right here in Texas with my husband."

"Is that a 'yes'?" His eyes widened with hope.

"What do you think?" She gave him a wide smile and pulled his mouth down to meet hers.

The rumble of heavy equipment floated in through the screen door.

She broke the kiss and angled her ear toward the sound. "If you never had any intention of bulldozing Sycamore House, what are those tractors doing outside?"

He turned her about-face and marched her through the kitchen to stand before the tall windows. In the backyard, Lacey and Mr. Latimer waved from inside a roped-off space marked with surveyor's pegs and yellow flags. "I guess those two wanted to be the first ones in the pool."

"Oh, Sam, a pool will be a treasure in the summer heat."

"You're all the treasure I need on this earth," he said, bending close to seal their love with a kiss.

* * * * *

Dear Reader,

Going home after a long absence can be an endearing or an unsettling experience. Finding yourself in old familiar places can make your heart skip a beat or your stomach churn. Hearing your name called by a voice from the past can invoke a memory of comfort or of confrontation. Moving backward in time, no matter the circumstances of your upbringing, is rarely without strong emotions.

Bound together as childhood friends and then shackled as adult business partners, Sam and Tara experienced all these feelings when they returned to their small hometown in *Sealed with a Kiss*. During a hot East Texas summer they realized that the dreams of youth were always possible, but only in God's timing.

As our children search for proof of God's existence, my siblings and I clearly see His divine fingerprints all over our lives. the more we submit to His will, the more He can bless us. We recall the trials He carried us through and the storms He gave us the courage to weather. And we realize we are each stronger because we've trusted His timing when ours was imperfect.

If you enjoyed Sam and Tara's journey, please let me hear from you at www.maenunn.com.

Until next time, let your light shine.

Mae Nunn

Send someone a little Inspiration this Easter with...

COUPON CODE: "V"

 & *Love Inspired*

Purchase any 3 different Love Inspired titles in March 2005 and collect the coupon codes inside each book to **receive $10 off the purchase of flowers and gifts from FTD.COM!**

To take advantage of this offer, simply go to www.ftd.com/loveinspired and enter the coupon codes (in any order) from each of the 3 books! Or call 1-800-SEND-FTD and give promo code 10069.

Happy Easter from Steeple Hill Books and FTD.COM!

Steeple Hill®

Don't forget— Mother's Day is just around the corner!

LOVE3

Take 2 inspirational love stories FREE!

PLUS get a FREE surprise gift!

Mail to Steeple Hill Reader Service™

In U.S.	In Canada
3010 Walden Ave.	P.O. Box 609
P.O. Box 1867	Fort Erie, Ontario
Buffalo, NY 14240-1867	L2A 5X3

YES! Please send me 2 free Love Inspired® novels and my free surprise gift. After receiving them, if I don't wish to receive anymore, I can return the shipping statement marked cancel. If I don't cancel, I will receive 4 brand-new novels every month, before they're available in stores! Bill me at the low price of $4.24 each in the U.S. and $4.74 each in Canada, plus 25¢ shipping and handling and applicable sales tax, if any*. That's the complete price and a savings of over 10% off the cover prices—quite a bargain! I understand that accepting the books and gift places me under no obligation ever to buy any books. I can always return a shipment and cancel at any time. Even if I never buy another book from Steeple Hill, the 2 free books and the surprise gift are mine to keep forever.

113 IDN DZ9M
313 IDN DZ9N

Name	(PLEASE PRINT)	
Address	Apt. No.	
City	State/Prov.	Zip/Postal Code

Not valid to current Love Inspired® subscribers.

Want to try two free books from another series?
Call 1-800-873-8635 or visit www.morefreebooks.com.

* Terms and prices are subject to change without notice. Sales tax applicable in New York. Canadian residents will be charged applicable provincial taxes and GST. All orders subject to approval. Offer limited to one per household.

® are registered trademarks owned and used by the trademark owner and or its licensee.

INTLI04R   ©2004 Steeple Hill

Love Inspired

THE McKASLIN CLAN

SERIES CONTINUES WITH...

SWEET BLESSINGS

BY

JILLIAN HART

Single mom Amy McKaslin welcomed newcomer Heath Murdock into her family diner after he'd shielded her from harm. And as the bighearted McKaslin clan and the close-knit Christian community rallied around him, the grief-ravaged drifter felt an awakening in his soul. Could the sweetest blessing of all be standing right before him?

The McKaslin Clan: Ensconced in a quaint mountain town overlooking the vast Montana plains, the McKaslins rejoice in the powerful bonds of faith, family...and forever love.

Don't miss SWEET BLESSINGS
On sale April 2005

Available at your favorite retail outlet.

www.SteepleHill.com

LISBJH

Love Inspired

THE FLANAGANS

SERIES CONTINUES WITH...

HERO DAD

BY

MARTA PERRY

Firefighter and single dad Seth Flanagan was looking
for a mother for his son. Then he met photojournalist
Julie Alexander. The introverted beauty made him
wonder if God was giving him a second chance. As he
watched his toddler son break through the barriers
around Julie's guarded heart, Seth realized he was ready
to love again. But would their budding relationship
be destroyed when he learned her real identity?

**The Flanagans: This fire-fighting family
must learn to stop fighting love.**

Don't miss HERO DAD
On sale April 2005

Available at your favorite retail outlet.

www.SteepleHill.com   LIHDMP

Love Inspired